SURVIVAL!

FOREST FIRE

HINCKLEY, MINNESOTA, 1894

K. DUEY AND K. A. BALE

ALADDIN PAPERBACKS

FOR THE WOMEN WHO TAUGHT US THE MEANING OF COURAGE:

ERMA L. KOSANOVICH
KATHERINE B. BALE
MARY E. PEERY

First Aladdin Paperbacks edition June 1999

Copyright © 1999 by Kathleen Duey and Karen A. Bale

Aladdin Paperbacks
An imprint of Simon & Schuster
Children's Publishing Division
1230 Avenue of the Americas
New York, NY 10020

The text for this book was set in Bembo.
Printed and bound in the United States of America
10 9 8 7 6 5 4 3 2 1

Library of Congress Cataloging-in-Publication Data
Duey, Kathleen.
Forest fire, Hinckley, Minnesota, 1894 / by K. Duey and K.A. Bale.
— 1st Aladdin Paperbacks ed.
p. cm. — (Survival! ; #10)
Summary: In 1894, Daniel and Carrie fight to survive as an uncontrollable
forest fire threatens to destroy their small Minnesota mill town.
ISBN 0-689-82928-0 (pbk.)
[1. Forest fires—Minnesota—Juvenile fiction. 2. Forest fires—Minnesota—Fiction.
3. Minnesota—Fiction.]
I. Bale, Karen A. II. Title. III. Series: Duey, Kathleen. Survival! ; bk. 10.
PZ7.D8694Fo 1999
[Fic]—dc21 99-29036
CIP AC

CHAPTER ONE

Daniel's eyes hurt, and he leaned on his broom for a moment. He looked down the long, planked boardwalk, squinting, wiping at the tears that wet his cheeks. The smoke had been bad most of the summer, but it seemed like it was getting worse.

Lifting his broom again, Daniel set back to work. He needed this job and he didn't want Mr. Greeley to see him loafing. This time of year, when the rains had gone and the streets had dried out, keeping the sidewalks in front of the Morrison Hotel clean was pretty easy work. There were dozens of boys who would snatch up the job in an instant if he got fired.

Working faster, Daniel leaned into the

familiar rhythm of sweeping. Mr. Greeley liked the planks clean for the morning crowds. Most of them were mill workers living in boarding-houses—but a few would be railroad men or sales agents. Mr. Greeley wanted the sidewalks spotless for them. He was always looking for ways to attract more business. Daniel glanced down the street. The sun was just coming up, the sunrise blurred and stained dirty orange from the smoke that hung in the sky.

Using long strokes that lifted the broom high, Daniel worked his way to the corner. He slowed, making sure the base of the streetlamp was swept free of the little, curved clods of dirt flung up from horses' hooves. Then he stepped past it and turned the corner, settling back into his broad, arm-swinging motion.

Once the wooden sidewalks were clean, Daniel turned his attention to the narrow planked walkways that started on either side of the corner streetlight and crossed the streets. This time of year it was possible to sweep them. Later, when rain and snow turned the whole town into a morass, the low, wooden pathways would be clotted with mud and slush.

As Daniel worked, the sky overhead got brighter with the eerie light that filtered through the smoke haze. The fires were getting closer, Daniel knew. The lumberjacks said there were areas where every stump was on fire, smoldering, glowing reddish at night.

Daniel noticed some of the planks in the center of the street were getting cracked from the weight of wagons rolling across them and would have to be replaced soon. The upkeep on the walks was constant, but the ladies of the town could at least get around without ruining their shoes and dresses. Hinckley was growing up, Grandma said.

Finishing up, Daniel heard a shout. Glancing back at the second-story windows of the Morrison, he saw a man leaning out, his hands cupped on either side of his mouth. When the man shouted a second time, there was an answer from down the block. Daniel saw the first of the day's mill hands straggling onto the street.

The sun was well up now, and Daniel knew that in minutes, the planked walk would be crowded with mill hands on their way to work. Then, at seven o'clock sharp, the whistle from Brennan's sawmill would blow, and the sidewalks would empty fast.

The next busy time would be around eight-thirty, when the businesses would begin to open up. That crowd would be almost all businessmen on their way to work—or to a saloon or the cigar store. Daniel liked to watch them walk past in their fine suits. The Eastern Minnesota railroad men had fine caps and walked with long, swinging strides toward the depot. But the St. Paul and Duluth line have the best conductor uniforms, Daniel thought, especially the passenger trains.

"Daniel Johansson! You going to lean on that broom all morning?"

The gruff voice startled Daniel into turning around, an excuse for his idleness forming in his mind. Then he saw that it was not Mr. Greeley. It was Cecil Robinson, and he was grinning.

"Good morning," Cecil called out, still using the raspy voice that had sounded like Mr. Greeley's. Daniel signaled for Cecil to wait, then sprinted into the lobby.

Mr. Greeley was talking to a man in a dark coat and tie, and Daniel had to wait, standing off to one side. It seemed like an eternity before Mr. Greeley finally faced him and reached into his pocket for the day's nickel. He flipped it through the air, and Daniel caught it neatly, making the tall, serious-natured man smile. "Be here in the morning?" Mr. Greeley asked.

"Yessir," Daniel sang out over his shoulder. He crossed the lobby and ducked through the narrow door that led to the service storeroom. He hung the broom from its hook, then spun around and hurried back outside.

Cecil grinned again when he saw him. "Race?"

Together they started down the street. They had barely gone half a block when the whistle of an Eastern Minnesota northbound freight sounded. Breathing hard, they stopped and turned to watch the train rush past, its engine leaving clouds of smelly steam behind. Daniel never got tired of watching the trains go through. There were sometimes ten or twelve a day now. Grandma said Hinckley was going to be a great city someday.

Cecil reached inside his shirt. "Here, Mr. Ericksen gave me some of the day-old cinnamon rolls."

Daniel's mouth watered, and he grinned at Cecil. "You have the best job in this whole town."

Cecil shrugged. "I guess, if you like getting up three hours before dawn."

"I would like that," Daniel said.

Cecil laughed at him. "It's the pastries and the pies you would like."

"I can't deny that," Daniel agreed, then took a huge bite of the roll Cecil had given him. His cheeks pouched like a squirrel's, he led the way south, then turned eastward, crossing streets midblock.

"Look at that."

Daniel turned to see Cecil gesturing. For some reason, a lumber wagon was coming right through the middle of town. The logs were stacked so high that the four-horse team looked too small, like toys hitched to the enormous load. The logs were untrimmed, with short, stubbed-off branches sticking out in every direction. The driver was cracking his whip, keeping the team at a labored, fast walk.

"He's new," Cecil said disparagingly.

Daniel nodded. "He'll catch heck if anyone tells Mr. Brennan he came this way."

"You already finish that roll?"

Daniel turned at Cecil's question, holding up his empty right hand. "I guess so," he answered. He waited, hoping Cecil would reach inside his shirt again, but he didn't.

The wagon was rumbling past now, and Daniel watched it go by.

"Look, Daniel," Cecil breathed.

Daniel was puzzled for a second, then understood. One of the logs was smoldering, a thin tendril of smoke rising. "It's like the whole country is on fire," Daniel said quietly.

"It scares me," Cecil admitted.

Daniel nodded, but didn't say anything out loud.

Cecil shrugged. "It's almost September. If it'd just rain, we'd be all right."

"The lumberjacks aren't worried," Daniel said. "And Grandma is convinced the cleared land inside the tracks will save us."

"My father isn't so sure," Cecil said.

"Do you want to get a bowl of ice cream later on when the parlor opens?" Daniel asked.

Cecil shook his head resolutely. "I'm saving for that bicycle."

Daniel felt another stab of envy. Cecil kept half his own wages to use for anything he wanted. Grandma didn't mind if Daniel spent a nickel once in a while, but she depended on his money—he would never be able to own a bicycle.

"Want to go out to the gravel pit for a while?" Cecil asked.

"Sure," Daniel said, glad to stop talking about the fires. There wasn't anything anyone could do about them, anyway.

CHAPTER TWO

"Carrie! Can you put that book down long enough to get breakfast?"

Carrie looked up at her father. She knew he didn't approve of her reading the medical books Dr. Legg gave her. In fact, he didn't approve of Dr. Inez Legg—or the fact that she ran her own hospital. He thought women were pushing their way into too many men's jobs.

"Carrie?"

She stood up and stretched, then started for the kitchen. In a few days, school would start, and it would be even harder to manage the house. She couldn't wait for Mama to come home. Her postcards said Grandmother Vaughn was getting better all the time.

Carrie tied her apron strings, then checked the fire. Humming, she lifted the lid on the oatmeal pot. It was simmering slowly, thick and bubbly. She stirred it and was relieved the bottom hadn't stuck. Once she started reading something that interested her, she was lost to the world. Mama always said the house could fall down around her and Carrie wouldn't so much as look up.

Taking clean bowls from the cupboard, Carrie glanced back into the parlor. Her father was standing at the window, staring out at the smoky sky.

"Are the fires getting worse?" Carrie asked, spooning a fat glob of fresh butter into each bowl of oatmeal. All summer long, Papa had been reassuring her. He was a volunteer fireman, after all, and he knew more than most people.

Papa turned toward her, smiling. "I don't think so. But I sure wish it would rain before your mother gets back."

Carrie nodded, pulling a tin of milk from the icebox. Then, she flipped the catch on the upper doors and looked in. The ice block was about half gone. She closed the compartment again, reminding herself to catch the iceman on his rounds next time she heard him coming.

Her father scraped back his chair and sank into it. He reached for the jar of molasses and stirred in enough to turn his oatmeal brown. As Carrie pulled out her own chair, he leaned to pick up the copy of the Hinckley *Enterprise* from the bake-table. He had already read every page, but he was in the habit of looking it over as he ate in the mornings. "Is there coffee?" he asked without looking up.

Carrie stood and went to the stove again. She had heated coffee from the night before. It would be bitter, and he would complain, but he would drink it. She poured a cup and blew at the steam to watch it disappear, then coil upward again.

"That's awful," Papa said after the first sip. He looked up from the paper. "Your mother is a saint when it comes to saving money and making ends meet, and I know she has taught you well," he added wryly. "Is there enough sugar in the house to make this drinkable?"

Carrie smiled and got the sugar bowl from the pantry for him. He winked as he dipped the spoon in three times, then stirred the coffee hard.

Carrie looked out the little kitchen window. "Will it burn closer to us, Papa?"

"Even if it does," he said evenly, "the volunteers can stop it before it hits town."

Carrie nodded. She had known he wouldn't tell her anything new, but she had wanted to hear it again. "So you think it's nothing to worry about?"

"No, Carrie, you know I'm concerned. But that new Waterous engine is a marvel, and the men are all well trained."

"I know, Papa, but—"

"And don't forget we came in second in a contest that included every fire department west of Chicago two years back. And John Craig is a steady man. We couldn't ask for a better fire chief."

"I'll try to stop worrying, then."

Papa nodded. "Just don't forget to stay alert. And if I can't get back here to make sure of it, remember I want you to—"

"Get on the first train out of town," Carrie finished for him.

He nodded. "I don't think any fire could

sweep across the cleared ground of the railroad right-of-ways. But if it does—"

"I could just ride Midnight straight away from the fires and I could—"

"No. I've told you before, you leave that damned horse where he is and hightail it to the Eastern Minnesota depot without looking back. They keep a schedule there, and if there's a St. Paul and Duluth train earlier, they'll send you across town."

Carrie nodded, crossing her fingers behind her back. She would not be going to either train depot. She would not leave Midnight. She slid into her chair again and stirred her own oatmeal.

The rattling of newspaper pages was the only sound in the kitchen for a few minutes. Then Papa lowered the *Enterprise* and tipped his cup to get the last of the sugary coffee. "I ought to be home by five or five-thirty. Olson wants me to help him move his wife's armoire." He grimaced. "She's always rearranging their furniture."

Carrie smiled. "I am going to the literary and music club this afternoon. Carla Nelson is going to sing for us."

Papa made a face. "I get enough of her in church. That woman could shatter windows."

Carrie bristled. "She is Mama's good friend, and she does a lot of good in this town."

"This town doesn't need a thin old maid lecturing the lumberjacks on drinking and gambling," Papa groused.

Carrie didn't answer. It was an old complaint. The women in Hinckley wanted a decent town fit for families to live in. They were always at odds with the rough-mannered men who cut the trees for the mill.

Papa didn't like the drinking and the fights every Saturday, but sometimes Carrie thought he disliked outspoken women even more. Whenever he and Mama argued about the club women trying to clean up the town, Papa said what they really needed was a tougher sheriff and more deputies. Sheriff Hawley did his best, but there were hundreds of lumberjacks and laborers.

Papa ran his hands through his hair, then reached for his hat and settled it on his head. He shrugged, adjusting the shoulders of his coat. Then he smiled at her. "Come straight home after the meeting and stick to the right-of-ways. Stay off the streets and away from the saloons. It's Saturday."

Carrie nodded. The lumberjacks raised a payday ruckus when they came to town. "I'll be careful, Pa."

He frowned. "I'll sure be glad when your mother comes home."

Carrie smiled at him again. "Me, too. I miss her."

"I do, too, but that's not what I meant. I'll be glad when she's here to keep an eye on you. I don't want you riding that horse of yours around town too much. And when you do, see that you ride like a lady."

Carrie watched him go out the door and turn left, heading toward the mill. He would be there long before the whistle blew at seven o'clock. He hated hurrying and he liked to have a little time with his friends.

Carrie sighed as she set about cleaning up. She was very particular about where she rode bareback, but someone must have seen her and told Papa. He hadn't talked about selling Midnight lately, and she wanted to make sure he never brought it up again. She would have to be more careful.

Carrie heated dishwater on the stove and used one of the slivers of lye soap to scrub the oatmeal pot. When she was finished, she rinsed out the bowls and washed her wooden spoons, then wiped up the tabletops. Humming again, she hung up her apron and dried her hands.

Carrie made quick work of the milking, then fed the chickens and the hog her father was fattening for Christmas. Going back inside, she set the egg basket on the kitchen worktable, then bustled around, making sure that the house was picked up. She had promised her mother she'd keep it neat.

Finally finished with her chores, she went out the back door and headed for the shed. Midnight whinnied and came to the fence. Carrie leaned forward, resting her cheek against his warm muzzle, inhaling the sweet hay smell of his breath. She opened the gate, and Midnight lowered his head so she could slip his halter on. She led him out to the hitch-rail. With quick, deft strokes, Carrie brushed the pasture dust out of Midnight's coal-black coat, then curried his mane and tail.

When she stood back, Midnight arched his

neck and sidled uneasily. "That smoke is still making you nervous, isn't it?" Carrie ran her hand down Midnight's neck, tugging at his mane. "It's bothering everyone."

Carrie rubbed Midnight's ears, and he angled his head, pressing his muzzle into her side. He closed his eyes, and she smiled. It had taken the big gelding a long time to trust her, but now that he did, he was as gentle as could be. She scratched his ears again, then stepped back slowly, smiling when he opened his eyes and lifted his head to look at her. "Want to go for a gallop?"

Midnight pricked his ears forward and shook his mane as though he were just now waking up for the day. Carrie went into the shed and pulled his bridle from its hook. As she gently worked the bit into Midnight's mouth, Carrie wished she could just change into the shirt and trousers she kept hidden out here. Then she could forget a saddle and ride bareback. But it was close to seven, and there would be people on the streets. If any of Papa's friends saw her riding astride, they would tell him and she would be in trouble again.

Carrie couldn't imagine not having Midnight, not being able to talk to him. It made her feel sick to think about not being able to ride. She was never happier than when she was galloping, the wind in her hair.

Sighing, Carrie went back into the shed and brought out a saddle blanket and the old sidesaddle Papa had gotten from Grandmother Vaughn. She positioned the blanket, then set the saddle on Midnight's back and tightened the cinch. Midnight lifted his head, shaking his mane. "I'll find somewhere to give you a good gallop today," Carrie promised. Midnight ducked his head, almost as if he were nodding, and it made Carrie laugh.

Papa had put an old barrel against the shed with a step stool beside it. Carrie led Midnight forward so that the gelding stood impatiently while she gathered her skirts and climbed up onto the barrel.

Turning sideways, Carrie lowered herself onto the saddle, quickly adjusting her skirts so that she could fit her legs under the curving leather saddletree. She tucked her right foot beneath her left calf, then bent to hold the single stirrup steady as she slid her left foot into it. Her shoe buttons clicked on the metal as she pulled her skirt down to cover her foot.

Carrie was barely settled in the saddle when the mill whistle blew. Startled, Midnight danced to one side, then reared, lashing his tail. Carrie sat him gracefully, keeping her hands low and her voice calm.

"You have heard that whistle a thousand times," she scolded Midnight as he came back down, shaking his head, his black mane stinging Carrie's hands. "Just settle down, Midnight," she scolded him again, pulling the gelding around and urging him into a spanking trot.

At the top of their lane, she guided Midnight eastward, toward the Old Government Road. It was empty now that the mill whistle had sounded and all the men were at work. Giving Midnight his head, she let him gallop out of town, enjoying the quick rhythm of his hooves on the dusty road.

Carrie kept Midnight at a gallop until she started down the incline that led to the Grindstone River Bridge. Then she pulled him back to a trot. He fought the bridle at first, tossing his head, but then slowed to a trot as they passed from solid ground to the echoing planks of the bridge.

There was no one on the far side, and Carrie let Midnight have his head again. This time he rose to a gallop, and Carrie leaned forward, keeping her weight centered, wishing she could ride without the awkward sidesaddle.

The road was sunbaked, and the wagon tracks were filled with powdery dust. Midnight's hooves kicked it into a pall that hung in the air behind them. It was already warming up. Carrie hoped it would be a little cooler today. She had bread to bake this afternoon. Mama always did it early in the morning, but Carrie did not want to give up her daily ride.

As Midnight slowed to a canter, Carrie could smell the stagnant odor of the swamp off to her right. They had had so little rain and the weather had been so hot all summer that even the swamp was drying up.

Reining in at last, Carrie turned Midnight back toward town and held him to a trot, his neck arched like a circus horse. She could tell that the smoke was bothering him more now that he was breathing hard, but he still wanted to run.

Carrie let Midnight gallop twice more, riding south to circle the gravel pit as she usually did. Today she didn't unsaddle him once the high bank of the Eastern Minnesota Railroad hid her from town. She was afraid to—even though that meant she couldn't let him out all the way.

Sidesaddles were not only awkward, they were dangerous. Midnight was surefooted, but there were old wagons out here, pieces of equipment, rusted and abandoned, and if he ever stumbled, she knew the sidesaddle could trap her beneath him.

At this slower pace, Midnight took longer to rid himself of his pasture-jitters. By the time he finally settled down, walking calmly when she reined him in, it was time to start home.

Carrie was glad Mama would be back before too long, but for reasons very different from her father's. Housework barely left her time to ride, and that meant Midnight was getting too little exercise.

Turning the corner back into their lane, she

glanced up at the weird, rouged sky. The smoke made everything look strange, and she was sick of the stinging in her eyes, the painful ache in her lungs. Unsaddling Midnight, Carrie tried not to worry about the fires, but it was impossible.

CHAPTER THREE

Blinking sweat from his eyes, Daniel chopped the kindling in a steady, smooth rhythm. He had finished early at the Morrison Hotel and now he was trying to get through his chores. He had promised Cecil that he would hurry so they could spend another afternoon out at the gravel pit.

Nels and Peter had challenged every boy in town to a slingshot contest in two weeks. Cecil had only had his slingshot a month or so, and he was still terrible. Daniel was pretty good, and he knew he had a chance. Nothing would make him happier than beating Peter Walsten.

Peter was always bragging about how good he was at everything. He bullied younger kids and picked on anyone who couldn't stand up to him. Nels Berg was good at almost everything—especially baseball—but he was a good loser and he never bragged.

"Daniel!"

He straightened up, leaving the ax in the chopping block. "What, Grandma?"

"When you're through with that firewood, I need some water in the kitchen."

"Sure thing," he called back. He wiped his forehead with his sleeve. It was heating up fast today. Everyone in town was sick of the heat and the dry weather. This year, everyone would be glad to see winter arrive.

Daniel lifted the ax again, slowly, in one smooth stroke the way Grandma had taught him. When he let it fall, he let the weight of the steel ax-head do most of the work. The kindling split evenly, flying out to land in the loose pile beside the block. Grandma was the best woman woodchopper who had ever lived, and the only reason she couldn't beat the men at it was that she was only four feet ten inches tall—and sixty-four years old.

Daniel carried the kindling into the kitchen, then almost ran to the pump, dumping the full prime can straight down the shaft. He filled the kitchen bucket and set it to one side quickly, turning to catch the last spurt in the prime can. He left it sitting by the pump—ready for next time.

"Do you need anything else before I go meet Cecil?" he asked as he came in the back door carrying the full bucket of fresh water.

Grandma turned to face him. "You up to anything I should know about?"

Daniel smiled at her. "No. Just practicing for a slingshot contest."

She grinned, her gold tooth flashing. "Just don't practice by any windows."

"We're going out by the gravel pit."

Grandma nodded. "Be back before dark?"

"I will," Daniel promised.

"Fried chicken tonight. And you know how Linquist is. If you want any, you'd best not be late."

Daniel went up the stairs, still smiling. Grandma's boardinghouse held only four boarders, all men. The rooms weren't fancy, and the house itself was old. It was Grandma's cooking that kept them from moving anywhere else.

Daniel walked past the boarders' doors, then climbed the steep stairs into the attic. It wasn't much past noon, but it was already as hot as an oven in his room. His bed was in one corner, near the small window. Grandma had sewn a curtain to cover the front of his makeshift closet, and he had an old dresser they had bought at a damaged freight sale. There was a long scratch in the top, but the drawers worked fine.

Reaching up to the highest shelf in his closet, he grabbed his slingshot and shoved it into his back pocket. Then he hurried downstairs and waved at Grandma as he went out the back door again.

Daniel left the yard at a run, startling the rooster and his harem into a clucking retreat. He sprinted through three yards, cutting across to the railroad tracks. The Eastern Minnesota line ran in a long curve that fronted the gravel pit. But Daniel didn't follow the rail bed through town. Instead, he ran straight for a ways, toward Rosehill Cemetery, then cut northward again so that he came out on the side of the gravel pit farthest from town.

Breathing hard, the sharp smell of smoke

grating at his throat and lungs, Daniel slowed down. It was so hot that he glanced longingly at the shallow, dirty water in the bottom of the gravel pit. Kids waded in it once in a while, but not very often. It was barely hip deep in the middle, and it stank.

Cecil was waiting for him. For the hundredth time, Daniel envied him. He had one part-time job and he was through by eight in the morning most days, summer and winter. His father worked at the mill, and his family could afford to let Cecil go to school regularly. Grandma tried to make do on her boarders' rents, and she wanted Daniel to go as often as possible. He had managed to learn to write and figure, but it was getting harder for him to miss work. His job at the Morrison paid the property taxes now, and Grandma needed his help more often at the boardinghouse, too.

"I remembered to bring the cans and I set up another target," Cecil said, greeting him. He gestured, and Daniel saw a broken wagon wheel propped up with a stick. Sitting on the rim was an old soup can. The label was torn, but Daniel could still see the words JOSEPH A. CAMPBELL

PRESERVE COMPANY. Grandma didn't believe in canned soup, but Cecil's mother sure did.

"How many paces?"

Daniel shrugged. "I'd say ten or twelve, at least. Peter and Nels won't take you seriously if you stand any closer than that."

Cecil nodded, a thoughtful frown on his face. "Maybe we should make it more like fifteen, make it harder on them."

"And on us, too," Daniel said.

Cecil laughed. "You're good enough to beat either one of them. I'll be in last place."

Daniel walked to the target and pivoted, facing away from it. Counting, he paced fifteen long steps, then turned back, scuffing a line on the ground. Then he pulled out his slingshot and bent to pick up a handful of roundish rocks.

Daniel's first shot was high, whizzing over the soup can. His second was a little low, clattering off the old metal wagon wheel. The third shot hit the can squarely enough to knock it off. He sprinted to set it up again, then turned back.

"My turn!" Cecil announced. Daniel stood aside as Cecil seated the first rock in the thick band of rubber and pulled his slingshot taut.

The shot missed high and wide, and Cecil muttered something under his breath. He loaded up again and shot once more. This time the rock skittered off at an angle. Without saying a word, Cecil tried again. This time the rock hit the ground just in front of the target.

"I'll never get good at this," Cecil said in disgust.

"I got my first slingshot when I was six," Daniel reminded him. Now watch." Daniel showed Cecil how to stiffen his wrist and sight over the top of the rock, keeping the band level with the target. "Like this." Daniel stepped in front of the target and pulled the band tight, then released the rock with a smooth motion.

Cecil tried again. This time his first shot grazed the top of the wagon wheel. His second came closer to the can. He turned to grin at Daniel. "I get it now, I think."

They practiced for a while longer, then began to walk, skipping rocks off the stagnant water in the pit. At the far end, they stopped in the sprawling muskmelon vines. Someone had planted them once; now they came up on their own.

Daniel found one ripe melon, and they shared it, juice dripping down their chins. A movement caught his eye, and he looked past Cecil. Someone was riding along the gravel pit. Daniel recognized the rider and the horse as Cecil turned to see what he was looking at.

"Is that Carrie Vaughn, girl jockey of Hinckley?" Cecil joked.

Daniel nodded. "She rides better than most boys."

Cecil laughed. "Not better than me."

Daniel eyed him. "No?"

Cecil blushed, then turned his head to hide it. "No. I ride pretty darn well." He lifted one hand to shade his eyes. "That horse of hers sure is fast. What does she call it again?"

"Midnight," Daniel answered. "Her father bought it from some relative of theirs who breeds racehorses in Minneapolis."

Cecil turned to stare at him. "How do you know?"

"She told me. I talk to her sometimes at school."

"You are hardly ever *there*."

Daniel turned to watch as Carrie put her

horse into a gallop, pounding along, her own hair and the horse's mane streaming out behind. A swirling wind kicked up, and fine sand rattled over the gravel. Daniel waded out of the melon vines, and Cecil followed.

Daniel waited for Cecil to say something more, but he didn't. He stood still as Carrie rode toward them like the wind. She reined in at last, the horse plunging to a dramatic stop.

"Hello!" she called.

Daniel touched his cap, wishing he had a real hat to tip.

"You sure can ride," Cecil blurted, then blushed when Daniel shot him an incredulous look.

Carrie lowered her eyes and thanked him for the compliment, then looked straight at Daniel. "I heard my father telling someone that your grandmother's boardinghouse was one of the best in town, Daniel."

Daniel grinned up at her. "I will pass that along to her. It'll please her no end." He took a step forward and cautiously reached out to pat Midnight. The gelding was still breathing hard, his coat wet with sweat, but he lowered his head and rubbed his jaw along Daniel's shoulder.

"He likes you."

"I like him," Daniel answered, and Carrie laughed.

Then her face became grave. "Look!" Daniel turned to follow Carrie's gesture. There was a black plume of smoke rising to the south. "Could that be Pokegama?"

Daniel nodded, and Cecil whistled softly. Neither one of them answered. Daniel stared at the smoke. Maybe it was from people's houses, not just trees burning. He had seen Pokegama once. The Eastern Minnesota tracks ran past the little town.

"It's farther away than that, I think," Cecil said quietly.

Daniel nodded. "Maybe as far away as somewhere south of Mora." Daniel stared at the distant smoke. Grandma kept saying it had to rain sometime. He just wished it would hurry.

CHAPTER FOUR

Carrie woke to the smell of smoke. She got up and dressed, pulling on her comfortable old blue skirt and white waist. She wanted to run out to the pasture and say good morning to Midnight. As strong as the odor of smoke was this morning, she knew he would be uneasy. But she could already hear her father getting up, so she made his breakfast instead.

"Stay close to home today," Papa said as he finished up his eggs and handed her the dirty plate. Carrie didn't answer, hoping he would say no more. She rinsed his plate, then turned around to find him looking at her. "I mean no riding."

Carrie felt her stomach tighten. She had

been so careful. She hadn't ridden astride in five days. No one could have seen her doing any more than gallop around the gravel pit, in a proper skirt and sidesaddle. For an instant she wondered if Cecil or Daniel had said something about her to her father, but she knew that neither of them would.

"I don't want you to ride at all for a while," Papa went on.

Carrie opened her mouth to defend herself, but Papa hushed her with a quick gesture.

"Nelson Henry was down in Mission Creek yesterday. He says the woods to the south are smoldering, every stump on fire and the ground as dry as a bone."

Carrie shook her head. "You could say the same for Hinckley, Papa. I was up by the swamp yesterday and—"

"Hear me out, Carrie," he interrupted. "The breeze has been steady from the southwest. I think we're in some danger."

"I know there could be a fire, Papa. But everyone says it won't come here."

He was shaking his head. "It could. There's no good reason to think Hinckley can't burn."

Carrie exhaled slowly. She had been telling herself for weeks that there was no real chance of the fires coming into the cleared land that surrounded the town.

Papa was frowning. "I wish I knew what was going to happen. If I was sure of a fire, I would put you on a train today."

"But, Midnight—"

"That fool horse should be the last of your concerns," Papa exploded.

Carrie realized that she had hurt her father deeply. "I mean," she said quickly, "you would come with me on the train, wouldn't you?"

Papa was glowering, shaking his head. "You know I wouldn't. I have to stay to fight the fire. There's an oath, Carrie. I gave my word when I volunteered."

Carrie felt terrible. "It's just that Midnight depends on me," she said quietly, hoping he would understand. If he did, he gave no sign.

"Just keep an eye on the smoke," he said, jamming his hat on.

"But, Papa—" Carrie began.

"Do as I say," he warned her. "If you hear the mill whistle blow the alarm, you'll know I won't be coming back to the house. You get yourself to a train station and use Mama's egg money to buy yourself a ticket to St. Paul. Tell your mother to stay there until you hear from me."

Carrie swallowed hard. "I will," she managed to say. Her father gave her a quick kiss on the cheek, then turned and went out the door. Carrie stared at it for a long time before she managed to get back to her chores.

Coming out of the privy, Daniel stared up at the sky. He turned a full circle, pausing when he came to face southwest. The smoke was so thick this morning that the sunrise was the color of blood.

Looking back toward the boardinghouse, Daniel saw Grandma pass the kitchen window. She would be starting the second round of breakfasts. Two of the boarders worked at the mill and were already gone. The other were sales agents and often slept in—sometimes until seven-thirty.

Going in the back door, Daniel walked into the kitchen. Grandma smiled at him and gestured for him to sit down at the table. "I forgot to ask last night: How is the slingshot practice going? Any hope for Cecil?"

Daniel shrugged as he pulled out a chair. "Maybe. It's too soon to tell."

Grandma laughed as she put a plate of hot-cakes in front of him. "That boy doesn't give up, at least."

Daniel reached for the honey can. He drizzled it over his pancakes while Grandma poured herself more coffee and sat across from him. He took one huge bite and chewed while she stirred cream into her coffee, then looked up. He swallowed, hoping she hadn't seen him stuffing his mouth.

"The smoke looks worse," he said, to keep her from focusing on his table manners.

"It can't get much worse," she responded, setting her cup down hard. "I've had a headache for two months, it seems like." She pressed her hand against her face.

"It's thicker, I think," Daniel said. "The whole sky looks muddy."

Grandma sat up straighter. "I heard two women talking about leaving yesterday," she said, and there was disdain in her voice. "Fools."

"I've heard men down around the Morrison saying the same thing. But no one seems to actually pack up and go."

Grandma sipped at her coffee. "That's because they all know that between the cleared land and that sump of a gravel pit, it isn't likely a fire would ever get started here."

"But they built that fireproof schoolhouse and—"

"They just like to spend civic money, Daniel. And it's a fine enough schoolhouse, I must admit."

Daniel shoved another bite of hotcakes into his mouth and washed it down with a draught of cold milk. It was the first glassful out of a new tin, and the cream was thick and sweet on top.

"Today's the new month," Grandma said, taking another sip of coffee. "Maybe September will bring us some rain."

"I hope so," Daniel said, to be polite. The truth was, he was sick of talking about the drought and the heat and the fire. No one who stayed at the Morrison seemed to be able to come up with any other line of small talk.

"Will you see Cecil today?"

Daniel tipped his head, chewing. "Maybe. If he can get away from his mother. She likes to have him do chores on Saturdays."

"Well, if you do," Grandma said, "tell him to ask his mother for her rhubarb cobbler recipe for me."

Daniel nodded. "I'll try to remember."

Grandma smiled. "If you forget, I will see her in church."

"Good morning," a booming voice rang out. Mr. Linquist ducked his head as he passed through the doorjamb.

Grandma got up and went to the stove. She pulled the skillet across the iron surface, centering it over the firebox. As she poured the first ladle full of batter into the hot grease, Mr. Rand came into the kitchen. He was a small man, and next to the tall, thin Mr. Linquist he looked even smaller.

"Smells good," Mr. Rand said, pulling out a chair and sitting down.

"It always smells good in here," Mr. Linquist agreed.

Grandma smiled and poured coffee for the two men.

Mr. Rand leaned forward. "You off to the hotel, Daniel?"

"No, sir, only the weekdays," Daniel said.

"When I was your age, I was working three jobs," Mr. Linquist volunteered. "I barely had time to sleep."

Daniel nodded slightly. He had heard all about Mr. Linquist's hardworking youth. They all had. Mr. Linquist still worked hard at his job as a sales agent for a saw and tool company. They had all heard about that, too.

"You gentlemen hungry?" Grandma asked, setting plates in front of the men. "There'll be more in a minute."

"Pass me the honey, Daniel," Mr. Linquist said before Mr. Rand had a chance to speak.

"Yes, sir," Daniel said, handing the sticky can across the table.

"I hear there's a baseball game planned for tomorrow," Mr. Rand said, unfolding his napkin. "You going to play, Daniel?"

"Baseball." Mr. Linquist's tone made the word sound like something awful. "No one should engage in such a frivolous activity on the Lord's day. I believe that—" Mr. Linquist was interrupted by a loud commotion in the street.

Daniel scraped back his chair and ran outside. A confused tangle of bawling cows stampeded down the lane.

"Lawson's cows again?" Grandma said, standing in the doorway behind him.

"Yes," Daniel said without turning.

"Why don't you go lend a hand? That man will suffer apoplexy chasing cows before he gives up and fixes his fences."

Daniel kicked at a stone and started to argue. He didn't like Mr. Lawson, and no matter how often he helped, the old man never so much as said thank you.

"Go on, Daniel," Grandma urged him. "Do your good deed for the day."

Daniel nodded glumly and started after the cows, picking up a stick as he went. He sprinted forward, veering to run parallel with the cows, jumping Mrs. Carlsen's hedge, then her rose bed. A thin, reedy eruption of curses let him know that Mr. Lawson had arrived on the scene, and he slowed enough to glance back. Mr. Lawson was brandishing a stick of kindling and promising the cows a bad ending if they didn't turn around and head home.

Marveling at the stubbornness it took for Mr. Lawson to consistently believe that his cows would one day learn to reason, Daniel sprinted again, darting out in front of them.

Waving his arms and shouting, Daniel startled the confused animals into a disorderly halt. "Mr. Lawson," he screeched at the top of his lungs. It took a few seconds, but the old man slowed, then stopped just behind his cows.

"Get out of the way!" Daniel shouted. He could see Mr. Lawson take offense at his impolite tone, but he seemed to get the gist of the message and moved to one side.

Daniel clucked at the cows, swinging his stick back and forth, slapping his leg with his free hand. Reluctantly, the cows sorted themselves out and began to amble back the way they had come.

Mr. Lawson fell in beside him and walked without speaking the half mile back to his pasture gate. Daniel ran to open it, and Mr. Lawson drove his cows through, then closed it. He walked off, headed toward his house, without so much as a backward glance.

"You're welcome, sir," Daniel shouted after him.

Mr. Lawson lifted one hand in an absent-minded salute, and Daniel shook his head. Then he looked up at the sky. The gray-blue haze that they had been used to for weeks really was darkening. Toward the southwest, it was very nearly black.

Daniel thought about going home, then hesitated. He got tired of listening to Mr. Linquist's advice on how to grow up correctly. If he could find something to do for an hour, the big man would be off on his Saturday errands.

Without thinking about where he was going, Daniel set out down the lane, wishing he had brought his slingshot. Cecil's aim was improving by the day, and he knew he had better make time for his own practice.

Passing the candy store, Daniel looked longingly at the penny chocolates in the window, then hurried on. He walked fast for another few blocks, then slowed when he heard a frantic whinnying from behind the Vaughn house.

Walking slowly, Daniel tried to see into the backyard, where Carrie kept her horse. It was

then he realized how dark the sky had gotten—
it was like trying to peer into the dusk. Guided
by the shrill whinnying and the sound of
Carrie's voice, he crossed the yard and stood
staring. The gate to the little pasture stood
open. Twenty feet outside it, Carrie was fighting to control her horse.

Midnight was on his hind legs, rearing, his
eyes edged in white. He squealed and turned,
fighting Carrie's grip on the rope. She jumped
back, getting clear of his hooves as he came
back down. Her voice was remarkably calm and
soft, and Daniel could only admire her nerve.
The horse was crazy with fear.

CHAPTER FIVE

Carrie was sure Midnight didn't want to hurt her, but she knew that he might. The smoke and the odd heaviness in the air this morning had scared him. She had been foolish to bring him out, she knew, but she had thought that walking him around the yard might calm him down. What he really needed was a good, long gallop.

Midnight reared again, striking at the air with his front hooves. Carrie stepped back and to her left, waiting until his hooves struck the ground again. Then, quickly, she moved farther to her left, pulling the lead hard, forcing Midnight to take a step.

Once she had him moving, Carrie walked fast, letting Midnight toss his mane and dance along, his eyes still wide, his nostrils flared. She had led him in a big circle around the garden twice by the time she noticed Daniel standing by the hedge.

"He sure is a beauty," he called out.

Carrie smiled at him, and Daniel walked toward her. "I was just trying to settle him down," she explained as he got closer. Midnight whinnied and lowered his head, looking at Daniel. "He really does like you," she said.

Daniel grinned. "I wish I had a horse like him."

Carrie didn't answer. Everyone knew how poor Daniel and his grandmother were. Their boardinghouse was too small to make them very much money.

A rooster crowed from a nearby yard, its cry echoing in the weird, still air. Midnight jerked his head up, and Daniel had to step back as he reared again. Carrie stayed clear of the gelding's lashing hooves and waited until he stood solidly on the ground once more. "He's so nervous," she said without turning to look at Daniel.

"Mr. Lawson's cows were running past our place an hour ago," Daniel told her.

"Must be the smoke is scaring all the animals."

"It's worse today," Carrie agreed. Then, as if it were trying to be contrary, the smoke shifted, and the sunlight poured through. The world was suddenly lit too brightly, slanted morning shadows appearing as if by magic.

Carrie heard Daniel take in a quick breath and knew that the sunlit world looked as strange to him as it did to her after weeks of the nearly constant haze of smoke. At that instant, a covey of partridges burst out of the hedge that bordered the garden. They scrambled through the short grass, spreading out, fluttering their wings. Two came so close to Midnight that he reared again.

Reacting too slowly, Carrie clutched at the rope, feeling it grate against her palms as Midnight jerked his head sideways, trying to get away from the commotion around his hooves. He kicked out, narrowly missing one of the birds, then whirled on his hind legs. Carrie could only cry out as the rope was pulled from her hands.

"Whoa!" Daniel shouted, trying to grab the lead as Midnight broke into a gallop and pounded past him.

"Midnight!" Carrie yelled, knowing that it was useless. The big black gelding slowed a little at the end of the lane, his head high and his eyes full of fear. The sky darkened abruptly again, plunging the world into a false dusk. Midnight whinnied, a high, panicked sound, then he galloped on.

Without thinking, Carrie ran after her horse. Midnight veered to the right, following the route they so often took on their morning rides. Carrie sprinted, lifting her skirt, but she could only glimpse Midnight as he turned off the road and headed out of town.

Carrie stumbled to a halt, her eyes stinging with tears. Only then did she remember that Daniel was there. He stood a little way off, breathing as hard as she was. Without saying a word to him, she began running again.

At the edge of town, Carrie had to slow down to catch her breath. Daniel had kept up, and when they reached the last corner, he gestured northward. "Would he just keep going that way?"

Miserable, Carrie shook her head. "I don't know."

"We should try to keep him in sight if we can," Daniel said.

Carrie nodded and began to run again, this time pacing herself, aware of the sharp scrape of the smoke in her lungs, the uncomfortable tightness of her bodice. Midnight slowed to a high-stepping trot as he turned up the Old Government Road, and she began to hope that she might catch him. Then a northbound freight came rumbling past, blowing its whistle, and he cantered again. The train rushed by, diminishing to a black speck in the distance. Carrie hoped there wouldn't be another train for a while.

"Will he cross the bridge?" Daniel shouted.

Carrie could not answer. She knew that Daniel was only trying to help. But she could not stand the idea of losing Midnight.

"Should I go back and try to borrow a horse from someone?" Daniel called.

Carrie slowed a little, thinking about it. Then she shook her head. Midnight was at least a half mile ahead of them now, but he had dropped back to a trot.

Carrie tried to keep running, but her feet

felt like lead and her skirts seemed to cling to her legs. She slowed to a fast walk, coughing on the acrid air.

Daniel fell back with her. "I could go tell your father," he said, timing the words between quick breaths.

"No!" Carrie said, whirling to face him. He looked so taken aback that she apologized. "He's worried about the fires. I wasn't supposed to leave for any reason, not even to go riding."

She saw Daniel's eyes narrow. "Your father is one of the volunteers, isn't he?"

Carrie nodded. "He said the fires could come through here."

"And burn Hinckley?"

Carrie shrugged. "That's what he said." She walked a little faster, her eyes still fixed on Midnight. He was grazing now, close to the side of the road. If she and Daniel spread out and stayed calm, one of them could probably get a grip on the dangling rope. She clenched her jaw. She had to catch Midnight, she just had to. For a terrible instant, Carrie imagined fire sweeping through, Midnight being burned by the flames. She shuddered, then pushed the image away.

It seemed to take forever to walk the distance to the bridge. Carrie kept her eyes glued on Midnight. He tossed his head as they approached, but he held his ground. "Don't startle him," she said in a low voice to Daniel.

"I'll be careful," he promised her. "You should be the one to try to get close." He dropped back a step as he spoke, and Carrie was grateful.

"Stay between him and the bridge," she told Daniel, and he nodded and veered northward.

"Time to go home, Midnight," Carrie said in a low, singsong voice. The black gelding stood watching her now, his lower jaw working the last mouthful of dried grass. Carrie advanced slowly, stopped, then took another step forward, talking quietly the whole time. Midnight faced her, his ears pricked forward. As she got closer, she could see that the wild look had gone out of his eyes. He had stepped on the rope and broken it, but a three-foot length still dangled from the halter. Carrie worked her way forward, then stopped again. She was almost close enough.

Hesitating, Carrie looked past her horse at Daniel. He was standing still, his hands and arms close to his body. Only his eyes betrayed the close attention he was paying to Midnight's every move.

"Whoa now, boy," she said softly, lifting her right hand so slowly that her muscles ached. She held her breath, watching Midnight's eyes. A flicker of the wildness showed for an instant, and her heart constricted. Then her fingers closed around the rope, and she exhaled, hoping he wouldn't rear. The lead rope was too short for her to hang on to if he did.

Midnight shook his head and nuzzled her. Then he allowed her to lead him forward a few steps, and she heard Daniel's quiet cheer. She looked up to see him grinning at her, and she smiled back. "Thanks for the help."

"I don't think you needed any," he answered. Careful not to spook Midnight, Daniel came forward. Carrie held the rope while he scratched Midnight's ears and patted his sweaty neck. Then they began the long walk back to town. Halfway there, the wind kicked up a little, and Carrie blinked at the stinging smoke it brought.

"Look," Daniel said abruptly. He pointed.

Carrie turned and realized that some of the smoke was coming from the mill yard. Some of the fresh-cut lumber was on fire. Men ran between the stacks, shouting orders and encouragement.

Carrie squinted, trying to spot her father, but could not. It looked like they had the fire almost under control.

Midnight tossed his head and pranced a little. "The fire's not coming here," Carrie murmured. "The mill hands will get it out. Papa will help them."

Carrie kept talking, making promises to Midnight that nothing would hurt him, knowing that her soothing words could not begin to erase his instinctive fear. Daniel walked beside her but not too close, and Carrie was glad that he had enough horse sense not to crowd Midnight when he was this nervous.

The road dust had coated Carrie's shoes and hem, and she knew that if Papa saw her, he would know she hadn't stayed home as she had promised. She quickened her pace. She needed to get home before his dinner break so she could clean up.

As they turned off the Old Government Road onto her lane, Carrie heard an odd, hollow, ringing sound at the outskirts of town. It took her several seconds to realize that it was the engine house gong.

"Oh, no," Daniel said quietly, and Carrie could only nod. The volunteer firemen were being called.

Daniel wondered abruptly how much time had gone by since he had left home. He looked upward, but it was impossible to spot the sun through the thick, gray smoke. He glanced at Carrie and was shocked at the pallor of her face. Then he remembered again that her father was a volunteer fireman. "Will he try to check on you at home before he goes to the engine house?"

Carrie stared straight ahead. "Maybe. I don't know. If he does—"

"Can you handle Midnight with just the halter and that broken lead rope?"

Carrie nodded, her lips pressed tightly together. "But if he sees me riding without the sidesaddle—"

Daniel frowned. "At least he would know you are all right."

Carrie pulled Midnight to a halt. Daniel clasped his hands together to give her a leg up. She thanked him, tightening the lead rope that would serve as a single rein. "I am afraid to have you ride double," she said, holding the frayed lead rope tightly as Midnight pranced sideways.

"Go on," Daniel told her, waving one hand to let her know he understood.

Carrie hesitated, then turned her horse and urged the big gelding into a gallop toward home. Daniel watched her round the corner and then he began to run.

CHAPTER SIX

Daniel hurried, scanning the horizon to the southwest. There was a billowing tower of black smoke rising upward now. Daniel ran, ignoring the sting of the smoky air in his lungs. He passed the bakery and the cigar store, dodging through the dinnertime crowds on the planked sidewalk. The breeze picked up, drying the sweat on his forehead as he went.

There were men in front of the town hall, and as Daniel slowed to a fast walk he could hear parts of their conversations over his own labored breathing. No one seemed to know how close the fire was, or whether or not they should try to leave town. All the sudden talk about leaving scared Daniel. There had been smoke most of the summer, but the debate had worn itself out weeks before. Now it was raging again.

Daniel wove his way through the crowd, jumping down off the boardwalk to dart diagonally across the street. He jumped back up onto the sidewalk on the other side, saw that it was less crowded for most of a block, and sprinted.

Then, at the next block, he had to slow down again. There were groups of men standing by the Morrison and, across the street, in front of Brennan's store. Some of them were talking. Some stood alone and silent. They were all looking toward the south.

As soon as he could, Daniel broke back into a heavy-footed run. His lungs ached, and he was coughing as he rounded the corner. He wove through the men standing along the front of the Morrison Hotel. Mr. Greeley was pacing back and forth, a scowl on his face. Daniel heard his boss calling to the cleaning girls to go back inside and was glad that Mr. Greeley turned and didn't see him. He had no intention of doing anything but going straight home. Grandma would need him.

In front of the St. Paul and Duluth depot were people standing in a loose group, their eyes glued to the northbound tracks. Daniel wasn't sure what time it was, but maybe the noon passenger train was late. He glanced back over his shoulder. He hadn't noticed big spires of smoke to the north, but it was so smoky, it was hard to see. Were the trains going to be able to get through? If they were, he wanted to get Grandma on the next one out of town, northbound or southbound, it made no difference.

The crowds thinned again across from Cowan's drugstore, but the Central Hotel had anxious-looking men standing in front of it. Passing through them, Daniel heard more bits and pieces of speculation. No one seemed to know whether people should try to leave town. Daniel heard one or two men arguing that Hinckley was the safest place to be. After all, the forests had been cleared all around the town.

Halfway down the next block, Daniel saw two families starting for the train station, their baggage in a pushcart. One was Nettie Andersen's—a girl he knew from school. She held the hands of her two younger brothers.

They were both crying loudly, and she had to drag them along. Her mother was crying, too, but more quietly. Daniel wanted to say something to Nettie, but he could not catch her eye. Without looking right or left, the whole family passed in silence as he ran on.

Winded and sweaty, nearly staggering as he coughed on the smoke, Daniel veered from the road across the front yard of the boardinghouse. The chickens scattered, and the cow bawled from her pen in the side yard.

Daniel flung open the back door and almost fell inside. Breathing hard, he glanced around the kitchen, then made his way through the dining room and up the back stairs. The door to Mr. Rand's room was standing open. He could hear his grandmother singing loudly, starting on the chorus of "Daisy Belle," nearly shouting the part about the bicycle built for two.

"Grandma!" he yelled, so that she could hear him over her own racket. "Come on, we have to get out of Hinckley."

She stopped singing and turned to face him. "What are you talking about?"

"Didn't you hear the gong?"

Grandma's eyes narrowed. "No. Where have you been? Did old man Lawson put you to work?"

Daniel shook his head. "I helped Carrie Vaughn catch her horse. Grandma, the gong sounded, and—"

"I didn't hear a thing." She pulled the top sheet off the bed, then bent over to untuck the bottom one.

Daniel shook his head angrily. "That's because you were singing too loud to hear anything. The fire is coming."

Grandma straightened. "They've been telling us that for two months." There was disgust in her voice.

"Grandma, I can see the smoke, and the mill is on fire. I—"

"We've had the smoke all summer, and they have put out fires at the mill two or three times."

"Mr. Vaughn told Carrie he thought there was a good chance—"

"A chance!" Grandma scoffed. "Even if it comes close, the cleared land will stop it. No fire is going to jump over the rail beds. There isn't enough for it to burn."

"That's not what Mr. Vaughn said."

Grandma paused, tipping her head to one side. "What exactly did he say?" she asked after a moment.

"I'm not positive," Daniel admitted. "But he told Carrie to stay home because he thought the fire could come our way."

Grandma shook her head. *"Could,"* she repeated.

"I think we should leave town," Daniel said, and it surprised him almost as much as it surprised his grandmother. Her mouth opened slightly.

"If it turns out to be a false alarm," Daniel heard himself adding, "then we can just come back."

"And how do we pay for these false-alarm tickets?"

Daniel looked at her. "But what if Mr. Vaughn is right, Grandma?"

She shook her head. "He can't be. If he was, you'd see everyone else packing up."

"I saw two families," Daniel told her.

She turned back to the bed, answering him over her shoulder. "Then let them figure out how to pay for the tickets. We can't afford it."

Angry at her stubbornness, even though he knew she was right about the money, Daniel whirled and ran back along the upstairs hall, pounding down the front stairs this time. He crossed the kitchen and banged out the back door. The instant he emerged, the gloomy gray of the smoke overhead began to lift. The heavy drifts of dark smoke separated, and the sunlight came through. It was the oddest, palest yellow that Daniel had ever seen. Everything looked off-kilter. He heard a woman scream in the distance, and the voices of men shouting somewhere over by the Catholic church.

The eerie amber light seemed to coat everything, falling like honey all around him. He looked up into the sky, half afraid of what he would see. The sun sparkled a few seconds more, then the smoke closed in again.

Carrie had been afraid to let Midnight gallop all out, but it had been hard to hold him back, too. He knew the way home and seemed to want to get there as fast as she did. Galloping around the last corner, she very nearly rode straight into a wagon full of children. The parents shouted as she hauled back on the halter rope. Midnight plunged to a halt amid screams and squeals.

Carrie sat her horse uneasily, breathing hard. She recognized the family. The man had started out working at the mill when they had come to town a year before. Now he works in the bakery, she thought. Sometimes she saw the woman shopping, her young children strung out behind her like ducklings.

"Watch where you're going!" the man shouted furiously, finding his voice at last.

"I'm sorry," Carrie shouted back. She was trembling, and so was Midnight. He whinnied and danced sideways.

"Get out of our way!" the woman shrieked.

Carrie guided Midnight aside and watched as the man whipped his horses back into a canter. He barely reined in for the corner, and the wagon tilted dangerously. Carrie bit her lip, watching them disappear into the smoke. There had been trunks in the wagon. They were leaving town.

As Carrie hesitated, the smoke ceiling

suddenly thinned, then parted, and the town before her was suddenly brightly lit, the sun shining a strange yellow color. Midnight's black coat looked gilded, and the road seemed laced with gold dust. The illusion lasted a few more seconds, then the smoke thickened and the sun's light became ruddy and soiled again.

Holding Midnight to a trot, Carrie rode the rest of the way home. She saw two more families standing in front of their homes with boxes and trunks full of their belongings. One couple was arguing fiercely. Carrie could hear them clearly. The wife wanted to stay; the husband thought they had better go immediately.

Carrie put Midnight back into the pasture, her thoughts wrestling with one another. Her father had told her to leave if the fire came. But if she left Midnight, what would happen to him? She thought about setting him loose, then starting for the depot. But what if he panicked and ran *toward* the fire?

Midnight cantered across the field, turning sharply at the far fence. His head was up, and he was obviously terrified. Helpless to make a decision, Carrie watched him, one hand pressed against her mouth.

"Carrie!"

She looked up to see her father running toward her. He had lost his hat, and his shirttail was half out. "I heard the gong, Papa!" she yelled out to him. "Is the fire coming?"

"I'm afraid it might," he shouted back, coming across the yard. When he stopped in front of her, he was breathing hard. "Chief Craig wants the volunteers," he said in a rush, then dragged in a long breath. "The whole swamp west of town is ablaze, and so is that side of the mill yard. I want you on the Eastern Minnesota one o'clock southbound—"

"What about Midnight?" Carrie interrupted, her eyes flooding. "I can't just leave him, Papa."

He gripped her shoulders, shaking her once, hard. "I said, get on the train." His voice was harsh.

She looked up at him, shocked. He had never spoken to her like this in his life.

"If anything happens to you," he said, lowering his voice, "your mother will never forgive me. Carrie, I have to *go*. Promise me."

Carrie started to cry, knowing it was the worst thing she could possibly do, but she couldn't help it. "Should I set him loose, Papa?"

Without hesitation, he nodded. "Yes. It'll give him a chance, at least."

Carrie nodded tearfully as her father handed her money for the train. "And don't take more than a few minutes' packing," he said, talking fast. "Wait at the station and don't leave for even a minute. Don't miss that train, Carrie." His face was grave, his eyes intense. She nodded. Then he turned and ran toward the engine house.

CHAPTER SEVEN

Carrie stared after her father for a moment, unable to move. She glanced at the pasture and saw that Midnight was still cantering aimlessly, turning sharply at the fence to double back. His coat was ruffled with sweat.

Forcing herself to hurry, Carrie ran into the house. She crossed the little parlor and went into her parents' bedroom. Her father's satchel was beneath the bed. She hurried to her own room and pulled her best dress and shoes from her dresser. Then she stuffed on top of them the quilt her grandmother had made. Heart pounding, she rummaged through her other drawers, adding a nightgown and an apron her mother had made. Then, satchel bulging, she stood up and looked around the room.

She had two dolls propped up on her bed pillows. She had loved them both and still did, even though she had outgrown them. She reached toward them, then stopped, midmotion. They would not fit in the satchel—and besides, there were more important things in the house to take.

Her knees trembling, Carrie went back into the parlor, scooping up the daguerreotype of her grandfather in his Union Army uniform and the carved ivory letter opener that Papa's mother had given him for a wedding gift. She whirled around and went to her mother's dresser. Luckily, her mother had taken the hairbrush set that had been part of her hope chest and had worn her silver earrings.

Running out the front door, Carrie stopped abruptly and turned back. There had to be things she was forgetting, things Papa would count on her to save. Frantically, she went through the house once more, trying hard to think. She grabbed Papa's Bible and her mother's tortoiseshell hair combs and put them in her bag. Then, refusing to look back, she went outside, closing the door behind herself.

Hands shaking, she set down the satchel and sprinted to the pasture gate. She opened it wide, then watched in anguish as Midnight ignored it, circling frantically inside the pasture. Picking up a handful of small stones, Carrie ran along the fence line, working her way past Midnight, not stopping until she was at the back fence. Then she started forward, shouting and waving her hands. Startled, Midnight plunged to a stop and faced her, tossing his head. She shooed him, tears streaming down her cheeks. "Go on," she pleaded with him. "Go on. Get as far from the smoke as you can."

Still, Midnight faced her, his ears pricked forward as though he couldn't believe she wanted him to go. Crying hard, she cocked her arm and threw one of the stones. Midnight's whole body reacted to the sudden sharp sting on his flank. He flinched, but held his ground.

Carrie raised her hand to throw another stone, then lowered it. Papa loved her and he was trying to protect her, but he was asking her to do something she could not do.

Moving forward slowly, Carrie came close to

Midnight, patting his neck. "I will be back in two minutes. You wait for me."

Carrie ran for the shed. She stopped just long enough to close the gate behind her. Midnight followed, tossing his head, stopping only when the front fence forced him to. She knew that if she opened it now, he might run. But she had already made her decision.

Carrie dashed through the planked door and went straight to the manger where she hid an old pair of trousers and a white shirt of her father's. The waistband was too big, but she buttoned on a pair of his suspenders, too. Emerging, she looked both ways, afraid someone would see her dressed like this. But the moment of caution passed quickly. She needed to ride like she had never ridden before, and wearing skirts might cost her her life—and maybe Midnight's.

Carrie ran back to the pasture gate and bridled her horse as quickly as she could, then led him close to the barrel. Struggling with the heavy satchel, she mounted. The wind was rising, and smoke was drifting like poisonous fog across the town.

Carrie clasped the satchel beneath her right arm and guided Midnight toward the Old Government Road—away from the Eastern Minnesota depot. As she urged her horse into a canter, she heard the sound of a train whistle in the distance.

Daniel stood, staring, his heart bounding like a rabbit's. The streets were filling up with billowing smoke. He could barely see the Eastern Minnesota water tank down by the tracks, and the sun was completely obscured.

"Johnny?" It was a woman's voice shouting, but Daniel couldn't see her. "Johnny!" she shouted again, and Daniel could hear the panic in her voice. An instant later, she appeared, a misty form in the thick smoke, her hair windblown and her apron dirty. She saw him and called, "Have you seen a little boy?"

Daniel shook his head. "No, ma'am."

She gripped his shoulders suddenly, peering into his face. "I can't find him. My husband is still at the mill, and I can't find my son."

Daniel had no idea how to answer her, but she didn't give him time, anyway. Angling away, back into the smoke, she disappeared, leaving only her anguished calls behind. Then the sound of her voice faded, too.

Daniel stared after her for a moment, startled when more forms began to take shape in the smoke. This time a whole family emerged. They were carrying bags and boxes, and the father pushed a trunk along the ground. If they saw Daniel, they made no sign. The mother was carrying an infant.

"Daniel!" The angry shout from inside the boardinghouse made Daniel spin around. It was Mr. Linquist, looming in the doorway. "Daniel, get in here! I need your help."

Reluctantly, Daniel went in, glancing back over his shoulder at the thickening smoke. How could Grandma insist they stay?

"Hurry up!" Mr. Linquist yelled.

Daniel followed him, trotting to keep up as Mr. Linquist's long stride carried him upstairs, then down the hall. Passing each room, Daniel looked for an open door, hoping to see Grandma still changing sheets. He had to talk her into leaving. There had to be some way they could get tickets for the train.

Maybe the conductor would let them—

"These cases are heavy," Mr. Linquist said, shattering Daniel's thoughts. "I'm going to need some help getting them downstairs."

Daniel glanced back down the hallway. Grandma was nowhere to be seen. She had probably gone down the back stairs to fill the laundry tubs.

"Did you hear me?"

"I need to find my grandmother first," Daniel said.

Mr. Linquist scowled. "I talked to her. She's set on staying right here. Says she's going to soak down the house if it gets too close."

Daniel nodded. She had been saying things like that for weeks. "Do you really think the town will burn?" Daniel asked impulsively.

Mr. Linquist nodded. "I do. And I intend to be on the first train that leaves. Help me carry these cases downstairs." With that, the tall, thin man hoisted the two biggest cases, jutting his chin out to indicate the two smaller ones. "Come on," he ordered, and went out into the hall.

Daniel hesitated a second more, then picked up the cases. Mr. Linquist kept glancing back, making sure Daniel was keeping up as they descended the stairs. At the bottom, Mr. Linquist led the way out the front door, his expression irritated.

"Where do you want these?" Daniel asked, looking around for a place to set the cases.

"I want them at the Eastern Minnesota depot," snapped Mr. Linquist.

Daniel stared at him. "I can't go that far. I have to—"

Mr. Linquist cut him off with an impatient gesture. "You have to talk that silly old woman into leaving, is that what you are about to say? Well, you can't. I already tried."

Daniel looked back toward the front door. He could hear his grandmother singing again. It sounded like she was in the kitchen now.

"Your whole generation is spoiled," Mr. Linquist said sharply. "When I was a boy, if one of my elders asked for help, I gave it. And I was polite about it, too."

Daniel found himself getting angry. "I think you are being unfair," he said, trying to hold his temper. If Mr. Linquist got upset enough, he might move out. Grandma would be devastated.

She hated having an empty room, even for a week or two—they couldn't afford the loss.

"Are you going to help me or not?" Mr. Linquist demanded.

"I'm sorry, sir," Daniel said. "I don't mean to be rude, but I really have to talk to my grandmother."

"I told you she won't leave!" Mr. Linquist exploded. "Now pick up those cases and let's get started."

Daniel shook his head. "I really can't—"

"Be still!" Mr. Linquist snapped. "You're spoiled rotten." He spat in disgust and looked past Daniel at the roiling smoke.

Daniel looked back toward the house once more. "If you will excuse me, sir," he began.

"What if I offered you twenty dollars?"

Daniel started to shake his head, then he realized what Mr. Linquist had said. Twenty dollars! That was enough to buy train tickets and get a hotel room if they had to. He stared at Mr. Linquist. "Do you mean that?"

Mr. Linquist laughed, and it was a harsh, bitter sound. "I said it, didn't I?"

Daniel nodded cautiously. "Then let's go,"

Mr. Linquist said. He picked up the bags and started across the yard, veering toward the street.

Daniel snatched up the two lighter cases and nearly ran to keep up. Mr. Linquist looked back twice, then just kept going, his long stride impossible to match.

There were wagons in the streets now, Daniel saw. Not many, but some people were leaving. The weird yellow light was gone, replaced by the gloomy false dusk from the smoke. The wind was blowing a little harder now, and the billows of white smoke that had rolled into Hinckley earlier seemed to thicken continuously.

Daniel could hear Mr. Linquist coughing quietly, the dry throat-clearing that had become habit for everyone in town. Sometimes the sound of coughing was the only way to know that they were not alone in the smoky street.

Daniel had to run a few steps now and then to keep from falling behind. He felt hot, as though it were July, not September. The air was so laden with smoke that it felt almost oily against his skin.

A block away from the depot, Daniel saw the Pails, walking like a family of bank robbers, their faces covered with scarves and bandannas. He longed for a piece of damp cloth to filter out some of the stinging smoke. He thought about his grandmother and how bad her headaches had been during the fire-plagued summer. She had to be in terrible pain right now. Maybe a scarf would help her, at least a little.

"Keep up, will you?" Mr. Linquist's voice was harsh, impatient.

Daniel hurried a few steps, then slowed again as Mr. Linquist led him down the planked walk that ran in front of the Catholic church. Daniel glanced at the closed doors. Father Lawlor would be with the volunteers at the engine house now. At the corner, Mr. Linquist stopped. Daniel nearly bumped into him. Cursing beneath his breath, Mr. Linquist glared at Daniel and started off again, crossing the street to head east.

At the end of the block, they passed the Presbyterian church. Without breaking stride, Mr. Linquist angled across the street, and for the first time Daniel saw the crowd of people standing just on the other side of the railroad tracks. There were families and mill hands, and lumberjacks who carried their saws and axes.

As Daniel stared at them, he heard a whistle. The train was coming. Mr. Linquist marched through the crowd, using his heavy cases to bull his way past people. Mr. Linquist walked up the line without asking permission or making apology when he nudged people aside. When he finally stopped, they were inside the depot, close to the ticket seller's window. Daniel followed but kept his head down, ashamed to be in the company of such a churlish man.

"Over there."

Daniel looked up to see Mr. Linquist indicating a clear area off to one side. Daniel carried the two lighter cases directly in front of his body to avoid bumping into people as he followed Mr. Linquist through the crowd.

Once Daniel had set the cases down, he turned expectantly toward Mr. Linquist. The tall man seemed not to notice him and pulled a handkerchief from his pocket, wiping at the sweat on his face. Daniel waited politely until he was finished. "I ought to go home now."

Mr. Linquist was bent over one of his cases and seemed not to hear.

"I really ought to be getting back to Grandma," Daniel said, a little louder.

Mr. Linquist looked up. "Then run along. No one is stopping you, son."

Daniel blinked, confused and uneasy. "I know that sir, I just—"

Mr. Linquist laughed, the same sharp, ugly sound as before. "You just what?"

"You said you would pay me, sir, and I—"

"I never said anything like that," Mr. Linquist interrupted.

Daniel was flabbergasted. He felt himself flushing and he had no idea what to say.

Mr. Linquist laughed, louder this time. "You should see your face, son."

Daniel clenched his fists. "That's dishonest."

Mr. Linquist rounded on him. "What are you accusing me of, young man?"

Daniel opened his mouth to speak, but the high wail of the general alarm cut him off. He stood rooted, staring at Mr. Linquist for another few seconds. Then he turned and ran, pushing his way back through the crowd.

CHAPTER EIGHT

Carrie was afraid. Things were getting worse. There was a stiff wind now, and it felt strangely warm. The smoke had gotten so thick she could barely see a few feet ahead. As much as she longed to hurry, she held Midnight to a trot, the satchel clutched in her right hand, the reins in her left.

It was dangerous to gallop down the Old Government Road now. Midnight couldn't see the ruts, filled with powdery dust this time of year. It would be too easy for him to miss a stride and break a leg. She cringed at the idea of Midnight having to be destroyed because she hurried out of her own fear.

Voices ahead of her made Carrie sit straighter, reining Midnight back to a walk as she strained to see through the smoke. It clawed at her throat and made her eyes stream tears that she had to keep blinking back to clear her vision.

A wagon finally emerged from the murk, and she saw Abigale Collier, a girl she knew from school, riding white-faced and anxious with her three brothers. Her parents sat side by side on the driver's bench. They lived a little ways outside of town, to the northwest.

"What are you doing out here alone, Carrie?" Abigale cried out, then coughed on the smoke.

Carrie couldn't answer. Midnight was dancing sideways, his neck bowed and taut. Carrie turned her head to let the wind push her hair back out of her face, keeping her eyes on Mr. Collier as he pulled in his team. He glared at her. "Clear the road, please, Carrie Vaughn," he rasped.

"Which way should I go, Mr. Collier?" she pleaded. "Where is it safe? Can I just stay on the road?"

"The only safe place tonight is a hundred miles from here," Mr. Collier snapped. He climbed down out of the wagon, setting the brake and handing his wife the reins. "Does your father know you're out here?"

"He told me to catch the train," Carrie said, and regretted it instantly.

Mr. Collier took a step forward. "Come back with us right now, then. That's where we're headed."

Carrie shook her head and pulled Midnight to one side. "Thank you," she said politely. "But I can't leave Midnight, and I—"

"There's no time to argue, young lady."

Carrie tried to pull Midnight around, but Mr. Collier was too fast for her. Reaching out, snake-quick, he made a lunge for the reins. The sudden movement startled Midnight, and he reared. Mr. Collier ducked to one side, and Carrie heard him curse beneath his breath. Then he lunged forward again.

This time, Midnight shied violently. Mr. Collier, off balance, one hand grasping for the reins, pitched sideways into the road. Midnight jerked the bit so hard that the reins slipped through Carrie's fingers, giving him the freedom he needed to whirl and gallop away.

Carrie managed to stay on, one hand tangled in Midnight's mane, the other clinging grimly to the slackened reins as he galloped. Carrie could hear Mr. Collier shouting, but she could not answer, nor could she seem to bring Midnight back under control, even once she had managed to tighten the reins.

The thick smoke scraped at her throat and lungs. Midnight's breathing was labored, too, his sides heaving, but he still would not stop. Terrified that he would stumble in the road ruts, Carrie managed to pull him to the side, at least, so that his pounding hooves fell on the shoulder of the road. She leaned low over his neck to get a better grip on the reins.

In that instant, three deer sprang into sight and leaped in arcs across the road so close, Carrie could see that one of them was literally on fire, wide patches of its coat smoldering. Plunging, Midnight swerved to miss them. For another three or four off-balance strides he was all right, but then he stumbled across the deep ruts in the road.

Carrie stayed on as Midnight pitched sideways, but when he crashed to his knees, she was jolted loose. There was an eternity of no sensation at all, then a pain in her right shoulder let her know that she had struck the ground. She rolled with the force of her fall, tumbling over the hard ground, coming to a stop on her back, staring up at the murky sky.

Suddenly, Midnight loomed above her, and she could see the reins trailing from his bridle to the ground. She lurched onto her side and reached for them, but they slid past, just beyond her grip. The sound of Midnight's hoofbeats dragged her to a sitting position just in time to see him disappear into the smoke.

Scrambling to her feet, ignoring the stab of pain in her right shoulder, Carrie stumbled into a run. "Midnight!" she shouted, knowing that it would do no good this time. He had been reluctant to leave the safety of his pasture, but out here, in the open, his instinct to flee danger would be stronger than anything else.

Unable to do more, she called out Midnight's name over and over as she veered off the road and ran across the uneven ground, following the sound of his hoofbeats. Her steps slowed gradually as she tired. When she stopped, gasping in painful breaths, she could no longer hear anything but the far-off whistle of a train.

Carrie stood for a long time, breathing hard, facing the direction Midnight had run. It was then, for the first time, that she realized she had lost the satchel. She began to cry, then coughed violently and doubled over. When she could finally breathe again, she straightened up, and an eerie disorientation clenched at her stomach. The wind had dropped. The smoke was so thick that she could not see more than a few feet.

Walking in baby steps first one way, then another, she finally found the road again. Pacing back and forth along it, she still could not locate the satchel. When she finally gave up searching for it, she stood, afraid to start off in either direction, unsure of which one would lead her back to town.

In the still air, the heat was oppressive, the smoke roiling around her. She forced herself to face what she thought was southward and was about to take her first step when the mill whistle sounded from behind her, blowing the general alarm.

Swallowing hard, Carrie whirled toward it, grateful tears filling her stinging eyes. She had been completely turned around and easily could have walked off into open country where no one would have been able to help her.

Crying, walking as fast as she could, Carrie started back toward town. She kept glancing back, wishing that she would hear hoofbeats—but the only sound was the pounding of her own heart.

Daniel hurried through the crowded depot. His face was flushed, and he was so angry he felt like he could explode. Mr. Linquist was a mean-hearted, dishonest man. He had never missed his rent, but he was often late in paying, and it always caused Grandma problems. And Daniel couldn't recall the last time he had heard Mr. Linquist thank Grandma for anything.

Emerging into the smoke that filled the streets, Daniel hesitated. The general alarm meant that the fire was close. He squinted and peered southward. That's where the wind had been coming from. It was rising again, a strong breeze now.

"The fire's coming up the St. Paul and Duluth road!" a gray-haired man shouted as he ran past the depot. "They need help down there!"

Daniel watched as several men started off at a run. The gray-haired man kept going, and Daniel could hear the shout being picked up by other voices. For a moment Daniel stood still, his thoughts spinning. If the man was right, the fire was within a half mile of the boarding-house.

Daniel began to run, zigzagging to avoid bumping into anyone. There were a few more people in the street now and they were silent, grim. Most of them were headed toward the depot, but a few were running in the same direction he was.

Daniel was seized by a sudden fit of coughing. He stumbled to a halt, trying to get his breath back, and noticed a wagon in front of Brennan's store. It was loaded high with what looked like empty water barrels. The driver whipped up his team, heading away from Brennan's at a hard trot. Daniel squinted, trying to see where the wagon was going, but he couldn't.

Daniel set off toward home again, walking

fast. The wagon was most likely just on its way out to Snake River Road. The volunteers had been out around the mill all morning long. Maybe the mill hands needed more barrels to carry water to fight the fire. With so many men to pitch in, they would probably have it out before long.

Crossing the road, Daniel saw that there was still a crowd of men standing in front of the Central Hotel. He slowed his pace, then sidled close to listen.

"If the wind comes up, it could sweep right through," a man with a loud, booming voice was saying. "I think—"

"But the Waterous engine—" someone interrupted him.

"That's still only one engine," a third voice put in.

"My brother-in-law is a volunteer," a tall man added. "He says that engine has two thousand feet of hose."

An old man leaning against the building front made a sound of incredulity. "Cripes!" He turned and spat in a perfect arc as the younger men quieted to hear what he had to say. "If a fire decides to come through Hinckley, no number of engines is going to stop it." He spat a second time. "I was in Chicago in seventy-one, and they had engines all over the city. They couldn't even slow it down."

"The Great Fire? What was it like?" someone asked him.

The old man made a whistling sound between his teeth. "I saw streets knee-deep in coals down around Bateham's shingle mill. And when Conley's Patch went up—"

"But that can't happen here," a man wearing a banker's suit said, cutting the old man off.

There was a chorus of agreement, and the talk splintered into a dozen small conversations. Daniel moved from one to the next, listening for a few seconds to three or four of them before he turned and set off again. He walked fast, but he was feeling less desperate now. Maybe Grandma was right. The men hardly seemed panicky about the fires.

As Daniel hurried along the planked walk, he lifted one arm to cover his nose and mouth—trying to keep the acrid smoke out. He saw several wagons, but only one of them was stacked with furniture and trunks.

In the doorways of the businesses he passed, he saw more men standing in loose circles, talking. He did not slow to listen to them. The nearly empty street told him what he needed to know: Most people were staying.

"Daniel!"

Daniel turned, startled. For a second he couldn't see anyone, but he had recognized the voice. "Cecil?"

"Over here." Cecil came out of the foglike smoke, his face cramped into an expression of worry. "Your grandmother told me you had taken off with Mr. Linquist. She said you might just end up getting on the train with him."

Daniel shook his head. "I wouldn't leave her here. I was trying to talk her into going—"

"But she won't," Cecil finished for him. "I talked to her about it. Daniel, you have to get her on that train."

Daniel shrugged. "I heard some men down by the Central. None of them was talking about leaving."

"My father says we're going as soon as he can get the stock loose and my mother's trunks loaded." Cecil glanced over his shoulder. "I should get back to help. I just wanted to give you this."

Daniel stared as Cecil reached into his trousers and pulled out his wallet. "Here." Cecil held out some bills. "For the train. Just don't tell your grandma where you got it."

"But what about your bicycle?"

"I'll get it someday."

"I'll pay you back."

Cecil nodded. "I know you will."

Daniel smiled, a weight lifting from his shoulders. "I've been trying to tell myself things would be all right here, but—"

"And maybe the fires will miss Hinckley," Cecil said. "But my father is sure they won't." He glanced over his shoulder again. "I have to get back."

Daniel grinned. "Thanks, Cecil. I'll see you on the train."

Cecil shook his hand. "Bring your slingshot. Maybe, if we end up staying a night or two in St. Paul, we can find an alley to practice in."

Daniel hesitated. Without meaning to, he glanced down at the bills Cecil had handed him.

"There's enough there, I think. Not for any-where fancy, but—"

"You're a real friend," Daniel interrupted, knowing that Grandma would be furious. She hated being indebted to anyone. He watched as Cecil turned around and loped off, vanishing into the white smoke after a step or two. Daniel set off at a run. Now that he had the money, Grandma would have to give in.

When Daniel crossed the boardinghouse yard, he was sweating. The door stood open, and for a moment he wondered if his grandmother had decided to leave after all. Then she came through the door carrying her laundry basket.

She saw him, and a look of irritation crossed her face. "You had me worried. Cecil was here looking for you, and I—"

"Put the sheets back inside," Daniel began, gesturing, but she cut him off.

"I will do nothing of the kind." She flounced out the doorway like an angry girl, turning her back on him as she headed for the clothesline. He ran to catch up, taking the heavy basket from her hands.

She gave it up, but frowned. "I can do that."

"I know," he said quickly, setting it down. Whether or not the laundry basket was too heavy for her was not the argument he wanted to start. "Grandma, I want to get us both on the train when it comes."

"I told you we don't have the money for that, and I—"

"I do," he said before she could get too wound up.

She glared at him. "And where would you have gotten that much money? We just paid the mortgage banker three days ago. You told me you'd given me all your wages."

"I did, Grandma," Daniel defended himself. "I didn't lie to you."

"Then where did the money come from?"

Daniel felt his cheeks redden and hoped that he was already flushed enough from the heat that she wouldn't notice. "Mr. Linquist paid me to help him carry his luggage to the station."

Grandma tipped her head, her eyes boring into his. "No man in his right mind would pay you that much for five minutes' work."

Daniel swallowed and looked past her, then forced himself to meet her steely eyes again.

"He was real scared about the fire and he was grateful for the help."

Grandma shook her head. "And so you took advantage of him being afraid?"

Daniel looked aside, knowing that this was one of those times when every word he said would only make things worse.

"I asked you a question," Grandma said.

Daniel was about to open his mouth and tell her the truth, but a clattering ruckus up the street made them both turn around. Coming out of the smoke like ghosts, four wagons rumbled past. Behind them was a crowd of men brandishing shovels and carrying buckets. They went past like a disorganized parade. Someone was shouting orders. Daniel heard the voice clearly, but could not spot whoever it was who was shouting.

"What's all this?" Grandma shouted. When no one answered her, she strode to the edge of the street and hollered her question again.

"Fire brigade, ma'am," a man shouted back at her.

An instant later, there was a second round of rumbling and clattering. This time, the famous

Waterous engine appeared out of the smoke. A flat wagon behind it carried the coiled hoses. Daniel stared as it went past.

"See that?" Grandma demanded. Her hands were on her hips. "They will stop any fire that comes this way."

Daniel nodded slowly, watching the men as they passed. He tried counting, but quickly gave it up. There were at least a hundred of them, maybe two hundred.

"Half of them are mill hands," Grandma said. Daniel nodded.

"So they know what they are doing," she said, emphasizing each word as though she were speaking to a little child.

"That doesn't mean that they can—"

"Yes, it does," Grandma disagreed. "It means an old woman who can't afford a train ride doesn't have to take one."

Daniel looked to the south, following the last of the men as they hurried to keep up with the engine. The smoke was thickest to the southwest, and it seemed to him like it was getting darker, too. The cottony white had a brownish tint now.

Through the smoke Daniel glimpsed an evil, reddish sparkling. He blinked and then could not see it again. Grandma had hoisted her basket of laundry on her hip, and he followed her to the clothesline.

Helping hang the clean, wet sheets, he kept looking past her, his heart thudding in his chest, but he couldn't see the sparkle again. He had probably imagined it. He felt the money in his pocket, and it reassured him. If they had to, they could catch the three-thirty train.

CHAPTER NINE

Carrie's right shoulder hurt, and she cradled her elbow in her left hand, trying to minimize the jarring of her footsteps. The smoke was awful, and her throat burned.

Papa was probably somewhere fighting the fire by now, as close to danger as he could possibly get. Every time she pictured him with flames torching the trees and underbrush around him, it made her heart ache. Imagining Midnight, panicked and galloping through the burning countryside, was almost as painful.

Carrie said a prayer for her father, then began adding smaller prayers to it, asking that Midnight be kept safe, too, and Daniel and Cecil. She remembered Abigale; then, using her prayers as a way to hold her own fear at bay, she worked her way through her school friends, then added Dr. Legg, who would be in the thick of things, trying to help.

By the time she heard the train whistle coming from north of town, on the St. Paul and Duluth tracks, she was so immersed in her praying that it took a few seconds for her to realize what it was. When she did, she started running. The train would catch up to her and pass her from behind, of course, but it would be in the depot for fifteen minutes or more before it went on south. If she could get to the depot fast enough, she could catch it.

The next blast of the train whistle was muted by the wind as Carrie raced along the dusty road. She kept glancing over her shoulder, trying to see through the smoke that bellied along the ground. She ignored the pain in her shoulder, desperate to make it to the depot before the train pulled out.

Running through the dense smoke, trying desperately to see, she veered off the road. She could hear the engine now, coming closer with every second that passed. If she could cut across to run parallel with the tracks, where the conductor could see her, he might wait a few extra minutes for her.

The train whistle sounded again. It was very close now, and she was sure the southbound train would overtake her soon. Gasping for breath, desperate to make the train, Carrie glanced back over her shoulder and blundered into a jagged tree stump. The pain was a quick shock that sent her spinning to one side, flailing with her sore arm, trying to keep her balance. She felt the crushing wrench in her ankle and she fell, crying out as the train rushed past.

Sprawling, she rolled onto her side, wincing when her right shoulder struck the dry, dusty ground. For a few seconds, Carrie lay still, listening to the sound of the train fade as it slowed for the depot in Hinckley. Then she forced herself to sit up.

Struggling to her feet, Carrie swayed back and forth for a moment, then tried to walk. Her ankle would barely hold her weight. Frightened and in pain, she limped along. She wasn't sure how far she was from the town. The smoke made it impossible to tell. But if she hurried, maybe she still had a chance to catch the train.

Her right shoulder was throbbing in time to her pulse.

"Keep going," she whispered between clenched teeth, forcing herself to take one step, then another. Lurching from side to side, Carrie managed to stay on her feet, but her progress was torturously slow.

The wind was picking back up, and the smoke drifted and pooled, never quite clearing enough for her to see how much farther she had to go. Still, Carrie did not allow herself to stop. She tried to hurry, but the all-aboard whistle rang out after a few minutes, and she heard the engine roar back to life. She stumbled to a halt, then sank slowly to the ground, crying. Then, after a long while, she managed to stop.

"There will be another train," she told herself between long, shuddery breaths. And she knew it was true. There were several passenger trains every day.

She swiped at her eyes and clambered upright again, wishing fiercely that she could tell how close the fire really was. She looked westward and saw a looming column of what looked like darker smoke. Was she opposite the mill yet? Was it burning down? How far did she still have to go to get back to town?

"Don't fall behind, Hans!"

The sound of the voice made Carrie look southward again. She could see shadowy forms off to her left. Was she somehow still that close to the Old Government Road? If these people had a wagon, maybe they would give her a ride into town. "Help me," she whispered, then managed to raise her voice to a hoarse shout. "Help me!"

Daniel heard the train engine. Then there was a loud blast of the whistle. "It's leaving!" he shouted at his grandmother.

She looked at him over the top of the clothesline as she smoothed out the wet sheets. "Then you can just stop trying to scare me to death," she told him. "It's too late, anyway."

"No, it isn't," Daniel snapped. He saw her face become stern at the tone of his voice. "I am not trying to be disrespectful, Grandma," he said. "But the fire is close now, and—"

"All right!" Grandma almost shouted. "That is about enough from you."

Daniel hesitated, knowing that if he tried to

argue much longer, she would go in the house and slam the door closed. "The fire is close," he said in a low voice. "I'm scared."

Grandma's eyes softened. "I am, too," she admitted.

"Then why wouldn't you just come with me to the station?"

"Tell me," she said evenly. "About the money."

"I did—" Daniel began, but she silenced him with an impatient gesture.

"The whole truth! Or don't open your mouth at all."

Daniel rocked back on his heels, trying to think fast, feeling his cheeks heat up. "It was—" he began again.

"Only the truth," Grandma reminded him.

He dropped his shoulders, giving in. "I ran into Cecil. He loaned it to me. He said they were packed up and ready to go."

Grandma made a soft sound of astonishment, then looked up at the smoke-hazed sky for a long moment before she met Daniel's eye again. "Mr. Robinson thinks we should leave?"

Daniel nodded. "He is taking his family out."

"To where?"

Daniel shook his head. "Away from here, that's all I know."

Grandma tilted her head to one side. "I respect that man's intelligence."

Daniel held his breath, not wanting to say a single word now that she was actually considering leaving.

"I suppose the three-thirty train would be soon enough."

Daniel nodded again, trying to keep a thoughtful expression on his face. "That should be soon enough, and it gives you time to pack."

"My trunk is up in the attic," Grandma said, reaching for another sheet.

"I'll get it," he said, then spun and ran for the house.

"I'm over here!" Carrie shouted into the hot wind. She couldn't see anything for the smoke. The pain in her ankle was increasing by the second. She longed to undo her boot buttons.

"Who is there?" a man's voice called.

"Carrie Vaughn," she answered. "My father works at the mill."

"I know you, Carrie Vaughn," came a boy's voice, and she recognized Hans Opgaard as he came toward her. Hans was the tallest boy in her class, and one of the oldest. His father kept him out most of the year to help on their dairy farm.

"What happened to you, girl?" Mr. Opgaard asked, half a step behind his son.

Carrie took a breath to answer, then realized that she didn't want to tell the whole story. If she did, she was afraid she would start crying.

"Where's your horse?" Hans asked. "Did you get thrown?" He was staring at her, an odd expression on his face.

Carrie was suddenly conscious of the trousers she had on, and blushed. "I was trying to ride fast—to get away from the fire."

"We are going to the swamp," Mr. Opgaard told her. "The fire is not so far away now."

Carrie glanced involuntarily toward town. "My father told me to get on the train." She crossed her fingers behind her back. It was almost true. She was ashamed to admit that she had planned to disobey her father.

"You would be safer with us," Mr. Opgaard

said. "You are going to be headed toward the worst of it if you go back to town." Carrie looked past him. Only then did she see that Mrs. Opgaard and Hans's three little sisters stood waiting behind him. Each of them carried a patchwork bag, made from scraps of the bright cloth that their mother favored.

"Come with us," Hans said.

Mr. Opgaard nodded. "The swamp should be safe, even if the fire comes straight on through."

Carrie hesitated. Suddenly, she was more afraid of being alone again than anything else. The sound of kind voices seemed to strip away the last of her courage.

"We can help you walk," Mrs. Opgaard said in her low, soft voice. Carrie fought an urge to cry. She was glad that her own mother wasn't here, wasn't in danger, but she missed her, too.

"Your father is a volunteer, isn't he?" Mr. Opgaard asked.

"Yes," Carrie told him.

"Is he with the others out by the water tower now?"

Carrie looked at him intently. "Is that where

they are fighting the fire? That close to town?"

Mr. Opgaard glanced to the west, his blond hair plastered to the side of his head by the hot wind. "And at the mill. It's hard to see now, but before noon there was a lot of smoke."

Carrie shifted her weight to ease her aching ankle and tried to think. If Papa was only a little ways south of town, and if the fire was impossible to stop, maybe he would be trying to get on the three-thirty train, too.

"We can wait no longer," Mr. Opgaard said quietly, nudging her out of her thoughts.

"You go on," Carrie told him. "I need to go back to town to find my father."

"If you can't, we will be just on the other side of the railroad bridge. There are a few places on this end where the water is deeper."

"Can you walk?" Hans asked.

Carrie took an experimental step. It still hurt, but she could stand it. "How much farther is it?" she asked him.

"Not far," he answered. "We could see the mill through the smoke just a few minutes ago."

Carrie tried to smile as Mr. Opgaard gathered his family and left, touching his hat in a polite salute. "Good luck, young lady," he called. Hans waved. Then they were gone, and Carrie was alone again.

She could not walk fast. Her ankle was swelling. Each step was short and painful, and she found herself glancing back over her shoulder, wondering if she should have gone to the swamp with the Opgaards.

Carrie was jarred from her thoughts when another set of ghostly figures walked toward her in the haze of smoke. This time no one spoke to her. It was three men, their hats pulled low over their foreheads, their strides long and purposeful.

Just behind them were two older women. They hurried along, mincing as they tried to keep the dust from their shoes.

As Carrie got closer to town, she encountered even more people. The sky was darkening now, and sometimes they were very nearly on top of her before she saw them at all in the wind-driven smoke. A few spoke, or offered her help, but most did not. Their faces were smudged with soot, their clothes speckled with ashes—and their eyes were narrowed and grim.

CHAPTER TEN

"Come *on!*" Daniel shouted up the stairs. The clock in the hall said three-thirty, but it usually ran slow unless Grandma reset it every day. Normally it didn't matter much. Today, it could make all the difference in the world.

Grandma had insisted on loading the trunk with everything from her mother's embroidered pillowcases to a packed supper. He glanced out the open door. The smoke was getting darker.

Daniel went outside, running from one end of the yard to the other. He released their chickens and the cow, then opened the shed door so even the mice could make it out if the fire came through.

"Grandma!" he shouted again when he was finished. He closed his eyes in relief when he heard her light footsteps on the stairs at last.

"Are you ready?" she asked.

Daniel bit his lip and simply nodded. She was wearing her best dress with her long, Sunday gloves. Her hat was positioned perfectly, the feathers jutting out over her right ear. He wondered if any of the other women would bother to dress up for this train ride. Probably some of them, he thought.

"Let's go," he said aloud.

Grandma nodded and led the way out the door. Daniel followed, dragging the trunk through the yard and into the road. The little wheels affixed to the bottom corners of the trunk were almost useless on the hard dirt. Daniel glanced around as they started off, wondering if Cecil's family had made it onto the early train. He hoped so.

The trunk was heavy, but he turned around, hooking his hands through the leather handle, lifting the end nearest him so that only the back wheels dragged through the dust.

"Look at that," Grandma said suddenly.

Daniel looked upward, following her gesture. A thick band of dark smoke was flowing through the sky above the town. Daniel blinked his watery eyes and traced the plume back down to the southwest. It was so thick on the ground that he couldn't tell for sure, but it looked like the source of the heavy smoke was close to town.

Daniel set down the trunk for a second and wiped his forehead while Grandma repositioned her hat. The wind was stiff now, but it was so hot that it didn't cool him at all. Looking over his shoulder at the darkening horizon, he put his hand back through the leather trunk handle and set off again. Grandma was coughing, but she kept up.

The center of town was crowded with people going every which way. Grandma walked beside Daniel as they turned the corner at the Morrison Hotel. At that instant, there was a round of shouts and screams behind them. The men who had been standing in front of the Morrison all turned to face the southwest. Daniel dropped the trunk handle instinctively, reaching out to take his grandmother's hand.

The smoke was darkening by the second, and the wind was getting even stronger. It was unnaturally hot, and the air was so dry that it hurt to pull in a long breath.

A clear shout made Daniel glance up the street again. It was Father Lawlor, his hair disheveled, his coattails flapping as he ran. He was yelling at the top of his lungs. Daniel felt his stomach tighten as the meaning of the priest's words became clear. "For heaven's sake, leave all you have!" Father Lawlor was shouting at the crowds. "Get to the gravel pit, run to the river! Hinckley will be destroyed."

Daniel looked back down the main street as he pulled Grandma forward. He saw flames on rooftops two blocks away, then, a few seconds later, only one block.

Struggling with her skirts, Grandma tried to run but couldn't. People on the street all around them were streaming past, running as fast as they could in every direction except toward the fire. Daniel heard a woman screaming somewhere close by, but couldn't see where she was.

His heart thudding against his ribs, Daniel pulled Grandma toward the center of the street, where there were fewer people. For a dozen more strides, it seemed to help. Without the crowds to dodge through, she could go much faster. Then she suddenly stumbled and fell. Daniel helped her up, seeing the terror in her eyes as she looked behind them.

He glanced backward. The Morrison was on fire now, the flames whipping over the walls, driven by the monstrous wind. It was picking up every second, lashing his hair across his forehead, so hot that it was almost burning his skin.

"You go on," Grandma said, shoving at him. "This is my fault. You were right, now go on."

"We can make it," Daniel yelled back at her. She shook her head, but he ignored her. He kept a tight grip on her hand, hurrying her along. They had a chance of making it if they could just get on a train.

From the depot at the end of the street, Daniel heard the train whistle blow. He saw that he wasn't the only one hoping to escape this way. A lot of people were sprinting down the street now, headed for the railroad platform.

Daniel struggled to keep his balance when Grandma lost hers again and again. Still looking toward the station, shielding his face from the heat of the fire that crackled on all sides now, he saw that the depot roof was aflame. There was a train waiting by the platform, though. But something was wrong with it. For a moment, with the hellish screaming of the wind and the swirl of sparks, he could not make sense of what he was seeing.

There was an engine at the head of the train, but it faced backward, hooked onto three freight cars that stood with their doors wide open. Joined to the last freight car was a caboose. Just behind it came four or five passenger coaches. He could see people scrambling to board. At the far end of the train, where the caboose should have been, was a second engine instead. It was facing backward as well.

Daniel steadied his grandmother, his eyes still glued to the strange train. Whoever had cobbled it together had not had use of the turntable, that much was obvious. Would it run? Daniel ducked his head, trying to look southward. The wind made it impossible. If the turntable and the water tank were on fire, he couldn't see the flames through the clouds of dark smoke.

Daniel tried to hurry, but Grandma, hobbled by her skirts and her age, couldn't go any faster. There were shouts, the words torn apart by the howling wind. People were crammed into the open freight cars, with more trying to squeeze their way aboard. Men stood with their hands out, helping stragglers climb up. The train blew its whistle—it was the long blast that indicated the conductor would shout the "all aboard" soon.

The flames were close and traveling fast. The heat was almost unbearable now. Daniel gasped in one painful breath after another, the hot air searing his lungs as he pulled Grandma along as fast as she could possibly manage. Grandma did her best, but he had to measure his pace to hers.

With the fire spinning and leaping behind them like a wild animal, Daniel could only keep running, holding Grandma's hand, almost dragging her now. The depot roof continued to burn.

At that instant, the engine at the head of the train began to back up, pulling the freight and passenger cars with it. The second engine belched a cloud of steam that was whipped to rags by the wind as the wheels whined and screeched on the rails until the two engines were working in tandem.

Daniel cried out, helpless to do anything but hold his grandmother upright and continue in what he knew was a futile race toward the train. On every side of them the buildings were exploding into flames. Daniel saw fire leaping like a predator, devouring the side wall of a two-story boardinghouse, exposing the neatly furnished rooms. For an instant the building stood, like a gigantic dollhouse. Then, it just seemed to melt, collapsing onto itself in an ashen heap.

Shielding his eyes from the heat, he could see that most of Hinckley was afire now. A block to the north, the big brick schoolhouse was burning, flames dancing in the heat-shattered windows.

There were men still hanging out of the freight car doors, reaching to help aboard anyone who could get close enough. But most of those who ran for the moving train could not. By the time Daniel and Grandma reached the end of the street, the train was gone, the second engine disappearing into the dusky wall of smoke.

Daniel glanced back. The flames were arching over the street behind him. He saw a woman running with her hair and clothes afire. Then he faced front again, sure that they had only one chance left to live.

Daniel did not hesitate. Veering northward, he skirted the howling flames that engulfed the depot building and put his arm around his grandmother, holding her upright. As he steadied her, helping her step over the railroad tracks just north of the station, he heard a chorus of screaming behind them. Grandma tried to turn, but Daniel forced her straight on, toward the gravel pit, the heat blistering at his back.

On the far side of the tracks, Daniel stumbled down the slope, staring at the shallow, stagnant water that filled the gravel pit below.

"Praise God!"

Daniel heard the shout and, for the first time, realized that he and Grandma were not alone. There were dozens of people wading into the water from all sides. The hellish wind, laden with sparks and cinders, roared overhead. The air was as hot as an oven, but the water, as they waded in, was blessedly cool.

"Where is it deepest?" Grandma asked, tugging at his sleeve.

Daniel gestured and angled toward the center, grateful for her good sense and her steadiness. He slapped at cinders that landed in his hair and hers, then bent to scoop up enough of the smelly water to douse them both.

Wading was hard for Grandma. She had to lean against him to keep from falling, but she never once slowed until they were standing in thigh-deep water. Then, without exchanging a word, they both sat down, letting the water rise to their chests.

Daniel closed his eyes for a moment, blissful as the water absorbed most of the heat from his clothes and skin. When he opened them, Grandma was still flushed an unnatural red, but she was splashing her burned cheeks with the tepid water.

Daniel looked out across the surface of the water toward the line of targets that he and Cecil had set up on the far side of the pit. There were farm animals walking single file toward the water, he noticed, then realized that many of them had already waded in. There were a number of cows, he saw, and a few pigs. Then his eyes fell on the proud arch of a horse's neck, and he pulled in a quick breath. It was Midnight, reins dangling from a loose bridle. Where was Carrie Vaughn?

The smoke was thickening north of town. Carrie heard screams and stumbled to a halt. Facing the hot wind, she strained to see. Her eyes streaming tears, she was astounded to realize that a crowd of people were running straight toward her.

Shouts of warning rang out. As the first of the runners passed, Carrie turned, trying to understand what they were saying, but she could not. Standing still, staring at the people as they rushed past, Carrie shifted her weight to ease her twisted ankle.

She searched the faces for someone she knew, not daring to hope that her father would be among them. Wherever he was, he would be fighting the fire, not running from it. Still, she could not keep herself from looking intently into every face as the crowd went past, most of them running headlong.

"The town's on fire!" a man yelled at her.

"Are the volunteers . . ." Carrie shouted, half turning to watch as the man sprinted past, her voice trailing off when she realized he had not heard her.

Without warning, a woman grabbed her arm and forced her to turn around, pulling her into a stumbling run. Pain shot from her ankle to her knee, and she tried to wrench free, but the woman held her fast. "Keep up!" the woman gasped. "Or we'll both die!"

"I thought I could make it to the station," Carrie managed to say.

"There won't be any more trains on these tracks. The St. Paul and Duluth telegrapher is dead."

"Thomas Dunn?" Carrie couldn't believe it. She shook her head, picturing the young man's friendly face. "Are you sure?"

"I saw the station collapse," the woman said, still pulling Carrie along. "He was still in there."

Behind them, Carrie could hear the labored breathing of dozens of people. They were all coughing, choking on the dense smoke.

"If we can make it to the river, we'll be all right," the woman said, twisting to look back toward town.

Carrie tried to answer, but the pain in her ankle was worse with every step. Struggling to stay upright, she looked back once more. The wall of black smoke was even denser now. The wind was a howling presence, and cinders stung her scalp and the back of her neck.

Propelled by the woman beside her, Carrie managed an uneven run. She kept her eyes down, watching the ground before her, afraid of falling. When they crossed the Old Government Road, she timed her steps so that she missed the deep ruts, doing her best to keep up.

"Come on!" the woman urged, coughing.

"I can't go faster," Carrie told her.

The woman didn't answer but she slowed her step a little, and Carrie was grateful. All around them, people were running, shouting back and forth in hoarse voices. The smoke made it impossible to see, and Carrie wondered how anyone knew which way they were headed. The Grindstone River and the swamp behind it were almost straight north of town, but it would be all too easy to slant eastward and not know it till they came to the Eastern Minnesota railroad tracks.

Suddenly, Carrie stumbled. Helpless to even break her fall, she felt herself crumpling, falling to one side. The woman helped her up, then spun around and ran on alone without a backward glance.

Carrie stood still for a few seconds, stunned, half expecting the woman to return. When she didn't, Carrie hobbled forward as best she could, truly frightened now, trying at least to keep the other runners in sight.

Through the roaring of the wind came a sound that Carrie recognized but didn't believe for a few seconds. Then it came again. Another train was blowing its whistle. This one was to the southeast! There was still an engine on the Eastern Minnesota track! Maybe that depot hadn't burned yet. Was it a southbound or a northbound? If it came north, maybe she could flag it down as it left town.

Her ankle sending shooting pains as high as her knee, Carrie turned toward the sound of the train whistle. The blinding smoke infuriated her.

Carrie glanced northward, instinctively looking in the direction of the river. Maybe it was foolish to risk trying to flag down the train. It might be smarter to get to the water as fast as she could. But there were trees and brush all along the Grindstone, and it wasn't very deep. For a second, an image of flaming trees and crackling twigs filled her mind. The river wasn't deep enough to protect anyone from this kind of fire.

Carrie hobbled forward again, setting her teeth against the pain in her ankle. The air was so hot it seared at her lungs as she fought to keep her precarious balance. Her stride was so lopsided that she had to hold her right arm out, aggravating her bruised shoulder. But the pain seemed to fade as she went on, buried beneath the oppressive weight of the heat.

The smoke was ink-black around Carrie when she heard the train whistle again. It startled her, and she very nearly fell, just managing to stagger to a halt.

Carrie started forward again, but more slowly. She was afraid that she might stumble into the tracks and fall in front of the steel wheels of the train. Again, she thought of her father and said a prayer for his safety. Looking back toward town as she had done so many times, Carrie caught her breath. She wiped the sweat and smoke from her eyes, unable to believe what she was seeing.

The smoke was so thick and dark that the shapes of the buildings were lost to her. But she could see the dancing sparkle of flames appear and disappear through it. A high-pitched wailing began, and she shuddered, unable to imagine what kinds of terror and pain could cause voices to sound so terrible.

"Keep my father safe," she pleaded, looking heavenward for an instant, then back at the billowing black cloud that concealed her town.

Slowing even more, sliding her feet forward one at a time, Carrie kept going, praying for the sound of the train whistle to come again. Finally, her left foot slid over the sharp-edged gravel that meant she had come to the rail bed. She knew, without taking another step, that she was only fifteen or so feet from the tracks themselves. A shrill whistle sounded, long and trailing. The train was coming.

CHAPTER ELEVEN

Daniel stared. Midnight was part of an unlikely gathering of people and animals spread across the bottom of the gravel pit. In the orange glow that lit the sky, he could see dogs and a few pigs pacing the perimeter, edging their way into the water.

There were groups of people strung from the base of the slope below the Eastern Minnesota tracks to the far end of the pit. There were two carriages, their wheels hub-deep in the water, bogged unevenly, the horses wild-eyed. Had they come straight down the steep embankment? A jumble of trunks and cases had been abandoned along the top of it, Daniel saw.

Daniel bailed more water over his head and splashed the back of Grandma's dress. Then he

glanced up again. The sky had become a glowing orange dome as the smoke trapped the light
from the fire, reflecting it back down. Daniel
heard a frightened whinny close by and turned.
Midnight had waded his way close to the center of the gravel pit. He was standing less than
thirty feet away now.

"What are you looking at?" Grandma
demanded, tugging at his sleeve.

"That horse," he said, leaning close so she
could hear him. He pointed.

"What about it?"

"It's Carrie Vaughn's gelding."

Grandma looked at him sharply. "Do you see
the girl?"

Daniel shook his head, squinting, wishing
that he *could* spot Carrie. He peered across the
ash-coated water, watching as Midnight tossed
his head. The trailing reins jounced with the
movement. One of them was broken off short.

Grandma bent forward again, splashing her
face, soaking the bodice of her dress. Daniel
took off his cap and used it to bail water over his
own head again. Then he clapped it back on.
The heat was unbelievable. The sky overhead

was lit like a madman's Fourth of July, the wind carrying shards of flaming wood out over the water.

A high-pitched squeal brought Daniel's gaze back down to the motley crowd of people and animals. He saw Midnight rear, a flaming shingle sliding off his bare back.

"Poor animal," Grandma shouted over the screaming wind.

Daniel leaned close so that she could hear his answer. "I should catch him."

"If the fire doesn't let up," Grandma shouted, "we might be glad to have a horse to use."

Daniel was glad that she saw some practical reason for him to help Midnight. He started to stand up, but Grandma pulled him close again. "If he fights you, leave him there. Don't get hurt."

Daniel nodded, an exaggerated gesture so she knew he had understood her over the whine of the wind. Then he got awkwardly to his feet. Turning around, he felt the heat hammering at him again.

Slogging through the water, his arms out for balance, Daniel approached Midnight slowly.

The gelding's head was up, his eyes wild. A shower of sparks exploded overhead, and as they floated downward, Daniel heard someone scream and the frenzied barking of a dog.

"Whoa, Midnight," Daniel shouted, his throat raw from the grating smoke. "Do you know me, fella? Let me get some water on you." Daniel took a step forward. Midnight eyed him suspiciously but did not move.

"Hold still now," Daniel went on. He held out his hand, edging forward. Midnight stood his ground, even when another shower of sparks burst over the railroad embankment and fanned out over the water.

Daniel clasped the reins in his left hand, and Midnight lowered his head, pushing his muzzle into Daniel's chest. Daniel could feel the big animal trembling. Daniel glanced back at Grandma, and she waved to show she was all right. Pulling off his hat, Daniel leaned sideways to lower it into the water. Straightening, he poured water over Midnight's back, quickly rubbing it in with the heel of his hand.

Midnight flinched, then sidled closer. Daniel dipped up more water, then took off his soaked jacket and laid it across Midnight's back like a misshapen saddle blanket. Working fast, he wet the horse's neck and face, then walked in a circle around him, splashing water over his whole coat. Then, leading Midnight slowly, he started back toward his grandmother.

Carrie stood, hunched against the hot wind. The train whistle sounded again.

"Can you see it?" The voice was so close that Carrie spun around, then gasped at the pain in her ankle. There was a young man standing beside her. Behind him was a woman, her face blackened with soot. She held a baby in her arms.

Carrie shook her head. "It's getting closer, though."

"We have to get out of here," the woman shouted, and Carrie heard a brittle timbre in her voice.

"Just calm down—" the young man yelled, reaching out to touch her face.

His wife batted his hand away, clutching the baby close. "You said we'd be safe."

The young man lowered his hand. "We will," he insisted.

As Carrie watched the false confidence pass from his face, a heavyset man came running out of the curtain of smoke, coughing and retching. After a few seconds, he straightened, wiping his mouth on his sleeve. "Has the train passed?"

Carrie shook her head, running her tongue across her lips. For the first time, she noticed they were blistered, and she wondered vaguely when it had happened.

"It hasn't?" the big man demanded, glaring at her. "Are you sure?" Just then, the whistle came again—from the direction of the depot. The big man nodded at Carrie, flashing a smile as though she had passed some sort of test.

A ferocious blast of wind made them all turn their backs. Carrie felt almost sick with heat. It was like standing too close to a coal fire.

"Oh, dear God," the woman shrieked. "We are going to die right here!" She began to sob.

Her husband put his arm around her, and Carrie saw him saying something close to her ear. Shuddering, the woman nodded as she pulled the baby's blanket closer around his flushed little face. Then she fixed her eyes on the track that led back toward Hinckley. Carrie followed the woman's gaze, praying that the train would come soon.

"How long ago did you first hear it?" the big man demanded.

Carrie started to answer him, then found that she really didn't know. It felt as though she had been standing beside these tracks half her life. The heat was relentless. The cloth of Carrie's trousers was flatiron hot, and she had to keep moving her legs to avoid scorching her skin. The shirt she wore was big for her, and when the wind flattened it against her body, the heat of the material was painful.

Through the howling of the wind, Carrie heard the faint sound of another train whistle somewhere far off to the northwest, above the mill. She turned toward it in surprise. She couldn't imagine any southbound engineer in his right mind coming up the Hinckley Big Hill and seeing the flame and smoke—and then deciding to come on into town.

"What train is that?" the big man demanded.

"The Number Four that goes to St. Paul," the young man shouted back. "Probably the engineer stopped north of town."

Carrie squeezed her eyes shut, trying to ease the stinging of the smoky wind. What difference did it make to her what trains she could hear or not hear? The fire was blazing all around them. The cleared railroad bed kept them from being set ablaze—but it couldn't save them from the terrible heat. They had to get away from here somehow.

Carrie's head was throbbing as though her blood had begun to boil. Her eyes ached, and she shut them again as the wind buffeted her. She was beginning to believe that she was going to die in this fire.

Thinking about her father made her start crying. The idea of Midnight galloping alone through the burning woods added to her misery. Carrie covered her face with her hands. It would be easy to give up. All she wanted was to lie down, to rest, to find someplace where the awful heat could not touch her.

Abruptly, Carrie thought about her mother. Mama would be worried to death when she heard that Hinckley had burned.

"Oh, my Lord!" the woman next to Carrie shouted. "There it is!"

Carrie looked up, narrowing her eyes against the windblown drifts of black smoke sweeping toward her. A blurred outline appeared, sharpening as it neared. Carrie rubbed at her eyes, trying to make sense of what she was seeing. The train was put together all wrong. Where the blunt face of the engine should have been there was only a vertical surface. Where were the rakelike steel bars of the cowcatcher?

"They've got it turned around," the big man shouted.

Carrie stared, trying to understand what he meant. Then, as the engine drew closer, crawling along the tracks, it became clear: The engine was turned around, backing up to pull the train.

"Look at that!" the woman yelled, lifting her baby to free one hand so that she could point at the odd-looking train.

Carrie watched, blinking and squinting as the train materialized out of the heavy smoke. The engine was reversed, and what followed made even less sense: A hodgepodge of cars, a caboose inexplicably in the middle, was overflowing with people. At the rear of the train was another engine, its cowcatcher protruding where the caboose should have been. The train eased toward them.

"Stop!" the big man shouted, stepping forward to wave his arms above his head. The younger man was only a half step behind. His wife clutched their baby, freeing one arm to join in.

Three people whom Carrie had not seen came out of nowhere and joined in the chorus. Carrie added her voice, the hot wind rising as if it were trying to cram it back down her throat.

"Stop for us!" the woman with the baby was sobbing. "Oh, dear God, please stop!"

The train seemed to slide soundlessly toward them, the huffing and clanging of the engine wiped away by the harsh roar of the wind. Carrie shouted along with the others, glancing back once to see that even more people were gathering beside the tracks now.

Without the engineer giving any sign that he had seen them, the backward engine slipped past them, going only a little faster than a man could run. Carrie listened for the sound of the brakes, then realized she would probably not be able to hear them. She could see the engineer and she cupped her hands around her mouth, turning to direct her pleas at him.

But the train did not stop. The reversed engine went past, then three freight cars did. People were jammed aboard, standing just inside the wide doors. Carrie could hear them shouting, their voices a shattered jumble in the wind. She stared helplessly, and they went past, so close that she could have taken four or five steps and touched them.

She lurched forward, following an impulse to run alongside the train to try to jump on. Then she caught herself, not because the pain in her ankle shot upward to her knee again but because she was as afraid of the steel wheels beneath the train as she was of the fire.

As she stood, shouting hoarsely, willing the engineer to stop, she realized that everyone had edged closer but no one was trying to leap aboard. The train had sped up slightly.

The woman behind Carrie began to wail. It was a high, keening note of despair and it penetrated the sound of the wind. Carrie heard another high voice take up the lament as the engine at the far end of the train rolled by. Through the windows, lit by the lantern above the cowcatcher, she could see the face of another engineer. He had turned away from them.

"They're leaving us!"

Carrie saw the big man raise his fist into the air. "They can't," the woman shouted, her voice rough. "They can't!"

Carrie glanced to see the big man still shaking his fist at the retreating cowcatcher on the second engine. She felt the last of her own hope draining away. She took a single step forward, then felt a blow on her shoulder and lurched to one side, her eyes still glued to the slowly receding train. When she managed to straighten up, she realized that the big man had pushed past her and was running up the track.

It took the young man only a few seconds to react. He nearly lifted his wife, turning her, beseeching her to run. Carrie hobbled forward a few steps, her ankle so painful that the very idea of running was almost more than she could bear. But she gritted her teeth and knew she had to try.

CHAPTER TWELVE

Daniel felt the bottom of the gravel pit slope slightly and he led Midnight forward into deeper water. The gelding was trembling and nervous as Daniel splashed him. The gravel pit was full of people now—a hundred, maybe more—most of them sitting down or lying in the water. Daniel could hear one man moaning, almost screaming. It took him a moment to follow the sound with his eyes. The man was with his family, it looked like. They were taking turns splashing water on him.

Glancing back every few seconds to make sure that Grandma was all right, Daniel tried to hurry. Only her head showed above the waterline. Daniel was pretty sure she was safe from the worst of the heat. Pausing only to douse himself, Daniel wet down the frightened horse, then led him forward very slowly.

The light was a nightmarish yellow-orange, still glaring down from the shifting ceiling of smoke. The glare was reflected in the water, the sheet of molten orange broken only by the heads and shoulders of those who had escaped the fury of the fire.

Daniel tugged at the reins, uneasy at leaving Grandma's side for so long. Midnight balked. "Come on," Daniel coaxed the gelding, half turning so that he could keep an eye on his grandmother. Looking past her for a second, Daniel could see flames above the embankment now. The tallest buildings were burning.

Midnight shook his mane, and Daniel tugged at the bridle again. He didn't really want to lead the horse too close to Grandma—an ember could make him shy dangerously. But he was afraid to be this far away from her, too.

"Grandma!" Daniel yelled. She was facing the railroad tracks, staring at the embankment that blocked their view of the town.

"Grandma!" he shrieked, and was grateful

when she finally turned. "I'm coming!" he yelled, then led Midnight toward her. This time the gelding cooperated. Grandma got to her feet as the horse approached.

"Stay under," Daniel shouted. His own clothing was nearly dry, and the heat was choking him.

"All right," Grandma shouted back, and he saw her sink back into the dirty water.

Daniel brought the horse as close as he dared, then sat down in the water long enough to rewet his clothing. He soaked his jacket once more and replaced it on Midnight's back, then turned to splash water over Grandma's shoulders.

"I'm all right," she yelled, craning her head back to meet his eyes. He saw her glance fearfully at Midnight, and he moved the horse a few steps away.

Just then, the flames that they had seen dancing higher than the embankment seemed to leap upward. They arced over the water, and Daniel was forced to sink back beneath the surface, clutching the bridle reins tightly. When he came up, he soaked his jacket and splashed water across Midnight's haunches. Then, glancing to make sure that his grandmother was all right, he dunked himself beneath the water again.

The heat overhead was increasing, and Daniel had to stay beneath the water until his breath gave out. When he came up, Midnight lowered his head, pushing his muzzle into Daniel's soaked shirt. Grandma was splashing water over her head and shoulders again and again. Daniel bailed frantically with his hat, the water steaming as it streamed through Midnight's black coat.

At first the flames seemed like flat bands of light, blurred by the smoke. Then, as they got closer, Daniel could see that they had ragged edges—more like torn cloth than fire.

People began to scream, and Daniel edged closer to his grandmother, one hand still tight on Midnight's reins. "Grandma!" he shouted.

She turned to face him, and he could see the orange light of the flames reflected in her eyes. It was unnerving, and he looked away from her for a moment. When he looked back, she was wetting her face and hair again.

Midnight shuddered as a shower of sparks settled on his skin. Daniel wet his jacket and replaced it on Midnight's back, using his hat to bail more water over himself and the terrified horse.

Daniel could barely believe the intensity of the heat. His skin dried in seconds, and then began to hurt. He fell into a routine of submerging himself, then standing up long enough to soak Midnight and keep an eye on Grandma. She was cupping water in her hands and sloshing it down over her face. Twice he saw her lean forward to soak her hair.

Through the whistling of the wind, Daniel heard a high-pitched barking. A dog was running along the edge of the water, its coat on fire. Daniel winced and took an involuntary step toward the unlucky animal. Then he caught himself and looked to make sure that his grandmother was still managing without his help. He dunked, wet Midnight down, then glanced at Grandma again.

Then he allowed himself to scan the water's edge. The dog was gone. The flames overhead curved closer, the searing heat like a pressing weight. Daniel heard people screaming again, and Midnight shrilled, tossing his head.

Then, glancing at Grandma, Daniel saw her slump forward. He dropped Midnight's reins and floundered toward her through the thigh-deep water. He could feel his own pulse hammering against his temples and in his throat. He grabbed Grandma's shoulders and hauled her above the water. Frantic, he shook her back and forth. "Grandma!" he shouted at her. "Grandma, are you all right?"

For an eternal instant, she remained limp in his grasp, her flushed face swollen with heat. Then her eyelids began to flutter, and he saw her lips moving. When she opened her eyes, she focused on his face, and Daniel let out a relieved breath.

The heat was unbearable now. Walking backward, holding both his grandmother's hands to steady her, he led her toward the deeper water, closer to Midnight.

The big gelding hadn't wandered but he was twitching the skin on his shoulders and flanks. One arm still around his grandmother, Daniel dipped his coat in the water, then replaced it.

Midnight lowered his head and began to paw, his broad hoof sending sprays of the cool water along his sides and belly.

Grandma flinched as Midnight soaked her, then steadied herself. Daniel kept his arm around her shoulders as they sat back down, the blessed relief from the heat spreading over his skin. He looked up at the sky once more. How long could the flames last? Was there anything left to burn?

Daniel scanned the bronzed surface of the water. People were hunched over, their faces contorted. Howling dogs stood along the edges of the gravel pit. There was a bawling cow off to Daniel's left. As he watched, its knees buckled and it fell.

Daniel forced himself to rise, dousing Midnight's skin. Then, the heat thudding inside his skull, he sank back into the water next to his grandmother. She glanced up long enough to shout a single word as the wind howled around them: "Pray!"

Carrie forced herself to keep going, a slow, uneven hobble along the railroad tracks. She could see the young man, his wife, and all the others ahead of her. Desperate not to fall farther behind, Carrie kept her eyes on the lantern that hung from the engine coupled to the back of the train.

The dark, choking smoke shifted and whirled, filled with drifting cinders. People on the platforms between the cars leaned outward, shouting encouragement. The train was going just fast enough that none of the runners could catch up.

Carrie began to despair. Her eyes were streaming with tears, her shoulders and scalp aching with the heat. She could not keep up with the train and the other people chasing it. The very air was ovenlike, and the wind scorched her raw cheeks. The smoke overhead had thickened until the sky was almost as dark as night.

When she saw flames framing the tracks ahead of her, she did not understand at first. When the truth became obvious, she slowed to a walk, sobbing in long breaths, doubling over to cough. The parallel spires of flame were the bridge's upright timbers—the Grindstone River Bridge was on fire.

As the train passed over the bridge, Carrie stumbled forward even more slowly, sure there was little point in fighting any longer to escape the flames.

"It's stopping!"

Carrie lifted her head, afraid to believe the words coming faintly through the roar of the wind.

"Hurry! It's stopping!"

Carrie hesitated between the burning timbers for a few seconds, then went on, placing her feet as carefully as she could, grateful the thick smoke hid the river below.

Terrified of falling, limping through a nightmare of soot and heat, Carrie had to overcome her pain and fear to keep going. On the far side of the bridge, she stumbled, then caught her balance and limped on, grateful to be back on solid ground. Looking up through the smoky darkness, she saw the train's lantern again and headed toward it.

"Carrie!"

She looked up, her eyes refusing to focus at first. Then she felt her father's arm around her shoulders as he guided her toward the train. She stumbled going up the steps, but he held her steady and led her into the crowded passenger coach. There was nowhere left to sit. Carrie grasped the back of a seat as the train began to move.

Carrie's father held her free hand tightly, and she could see tears of relief in his eyes. She wanted to cry, too, but she couldn't. She was still trying to believe he was real, that the train had really stopped and she was not going to die after all.

For the next hour the train passed between burning forests. The flames licked and leaped at the windows. The metal floor beneath her feet was hot. The weird orange light made deep shadows on her father's face, and she could only stare and cling to his hand.

"We're coming out of it," Papa said finally. Carrie bent to look out the window and accidently touched the glass with her forehead. It was so hot, the sweat on her forehead sizzled as though she had touched a frying pan. The unexpected pain shocked her into tears.

Carrie tried not to cry, but the sobs that welled up inside her were uncontrollable, shaking her whole body. She leaned against her father, and he held her tightly, stroking her hair, telling her over and over that she had been brave and that the worst was over.

CHAPTER THIRTEEN

"Daniel!"

He stopped midmotion, one hand on Midnight's reins, the other holding his cap. Water trickled from his hat as he turned to face his grandmother. She had been silent so long that the sound of her voice seemed odd.

"It's passed us," she said, and he realized that she wasn't shouting, that the terrible wind had eased. She pointed at the embankment.

Feeling stunned, he followed her gesture. The slope was littered with cases and trunks. He saw a dog sniffing at something, then it ran off, limping. Daniel glanced back across the pit. Many of the people were standing up, stiff and slow. The strange gold-orange light of the fire shone less brightly now, and Daniel looked overhead, startled to see that the flames had receded. Where the dark smoke parted, there were streaks of sky—graying now with dusk. The whole day had passed, he realized. It would soon be nighttime.

"Help me up, Daniel," Grandma said.

He dropped the reins. Midnight was standing docilely now, his head low. Grandma let Daniel lift her from behind, then stood, swaying on her feet.

A babble of voices rose from the far edge of the pit, and Daniel saw people carrying what looked like melons. His mouth flooded with saliva.

The next few hours passed in a dreamlike procession. Someone had managed to milk a cow. Daniel had begged for some milk for Grandma, using a hollowed melon half as an oversized cup. No one talked much, and Daniel knew he looked as exhausted and hollow-eyed as anyone.

He heard a woman scream and he turned to see the body of a man floating in the water. Grandma made a sound of sympathy, and Daniel saw tears come into her eyes as a group of people gathered around the body. Midnight nudged his shoulder, and he turned, grateful for the distraction.

"There's Chief Craig," Grandma said.

Daniel turned to look at the fire chief and saw an expression of pure misery on his face. Glancing around, Daniel recognized the Reverend Knudsen and the mayor among the exhausted faces.

Daniel and Grandma straggled up out of the gravel pit, joining the ragged parade of people who headed for the unburned roundhouse. Grandma walked a little apart, still leery of Midnight. His coat was matted with silt from the muddy water, but Daniel was pretty sure he hadn't been burned.

"The worst is over," Grandma said as they topped the embankment.

Daniel nodded as he led Midnight through the maze of trunks and cases. It was true. The difference was that there was very little left to burn, and the wind had dropped. Crossing the street, he saw ashen shapes that he knew were the bodies of people who had not made it to safety. He glanced up at Grandma. She had covered her mouth and turned away from the terrible sight.

A little farther on, they could see the pile of blackened rubble that had been the boarding-house. Grandma cried, but she shook her head when he stopped Midnight and tried to comfort her.

"You are alive, and so am I," she managed to say between shuddering breaths. "That's more than enough." Daniel stood still, unsure of what to do or say. After a moment, wiping her eyes, Grandma smiled at him. It was a giddy, little-girl smile, and he found himself returning it, almost overcome by an unreasoning joy that he knew wouldn't last. Still, she was right. They were alive!

Carrie kept glancing at her father as he urged the hired team along the Old Government Road. It had been a week since the fire, but it seemed shorter to Carrie. Her ankle was a little better, but she was still tired and every night she had awakened, her heart thumping, afraid that the fire was about to catch her.

"You're going to feel better once Mama can take care of you," Papa said for the tenth time since they had set out from Duluth. He was sitting hunched over, the buggy whip in his right hand. He was impatient to see Mama, too, Carrie knew.

It was strange to come back through the blackened hills. There were parts of the train ride out of Hinckley that Carrie could not remember. Papa told her that she had passed out, standing up. The last seven days in Duluth had seemed both endless, and short. Papa had wired Mama in St. Paul, and her reply had consisted of four words: THANK GOD! COME SOON.

Carrie hadn't wanted to come through Hinckley at first, but so many of the railroad bridges were out that the dirt and gravel roads were the only way to get between the remaining train depots. Papa said there were places where the fire had actually melted the rails, and liquid steel was running across the ground. He had also told her that the governor was determined to rebuild Hinckley, and that the mill would reopen as soon as possible. Papa was just as determined that they would move back as soon as there were houses built to rent.

Coming up the Hinckley Big Hill, Carrie held her breath, knowing she would cry the minute she saw the town gone. She couldn't help but hope that Midnight had somehow gotten through the fire, but she knew it was not likely. All the way down from Duluth they had seen dead deer and rabbits. And Papa said that more than two hundred people in Hinckley had been killed.

Just as they crested the hill, Papa reached out and took Carrie's hand. She gasped and heard him draw in a quick breath, too. There wasn't much left of their little town but the round-house and the water tower—and the battered and blackened shell of the new schoolhouse. Stunned, Carrie sat rigidly as they crossed the bridge and followed the Old Government Road straight through the middle of town.

There were a few tents set up, and Carrie saw people and carriages in the distance and realized it was probably a funeral service out at Rosehill Cemetery. Her eyes filling with tears, she wondered how many of her friends were already buried there. Sadness washed over her, and she heard her father clear his throat and knew he was trying not to cry. She stared at the horses' backs, wishing Papa would make them gallop, leaving Hinckley far behind.

"There's one friend who made it," Papa said quietly.

Carrie looked up and saw Daniel, carrying an armload of what looked like splintered wood. She stood on the footrest and shouted his name. Daniel jerked around, saw her, and ran toward the wagon as Papa reined in.

Papa didn't say a word when Daniel leaped up onto the sideboard and kissed her on the cheek. "Good to see you, sir," Daniel said, leaning across to shake Papa's hand. Papa was smiling broadly.

Carrie found herself shivering, even though the day was hot. "I was afraid you were dead."

Daniel nodded, and she knew he had been afraid for her, too. Carrie hesitated, searching his eyes. "Your grandmother?"

"She's as good as new, except her hair got burned."

Carrie balled her hands into fists. "And Cecil?"

Daniel smiled. "He left on one of the early trains. His family should be fine."

Carrie exhaled again. She didn't want to ask about anyone else. Not yet.

"Are you moving back here?" Daniel asked, looking past her at her father. "There's a man here who says there'll be a hundred houses built by next year."

"We plan to come back," Papa said without hesitating.

"Grandma feels the same. She got hired on as a cook for the relief workers."

"So you are making out all right?" Papa asked.

Daniel nodded. "Can Carrie come with me to see Grandma?"

Papa turned to her. "Can you walk well enough?"

Carrie nodded. "If I go slow."

"Don't hurry. I'll go down to talk to the relief workers for a few minutes," Papa said.

Carrie got down from the wagon, leaning on Daniel's arm until she had both feet on the ground. Then she followed him, holding her new skirt above the blackened earth, her eyes sweeping across the ruined town. He led her slowly along the St. Paul and Duluth tracks, and she could see how misshapen they were in places. The gravel pit looked stark and strange, visible now from where she stood—with no buildings standing to block her view.

"I have a surprise for you," Daniel said as they came around the water tank.

Carrie had been staring at the gathering of people at the cemetery. Now, she looked back at him, trying to smile. "What?"

Daniel gestured. There, in the little unburned clearing, Carrie saw a row of tents and a number of people standing, talking. She didn't recognize any of them. She glanced at Daniel again.

"On the far side," he said. "Beyond the tents."

Carrie looked once more. This time, she saw the tall black gelding tethered to a half-burned tree. Dizzy with happiness, she hugged Daniel, then let him help her walk across the ash-covered ground. Midnight whinnied when he saw her coming, straining at the rope until she was close. Then he lowered his head for her to scratch his ears.

"Thank you." Carrie looked at Daniel, tears stinging her eyes, wishing she could manage to say something more. But she was both happier and sadder than she had ever been in her life, and she began to cry.

Sometimes one day can change a life forever

American Diaries

Different girls, living in different periods of America's past,
reveal their hearts' secrets in the pages of their diaries.
Each one faces a challenge that will change her life forever.
Don't miss any of their stories:

#1 ❧ Sarah Anne Hartford ❧

#2 ❧ Emma Eileen Grove ❧

#3 ❧ Anisett Lundberg ❧

#4 ❧ Mary Alice Peale ❧

#5 ❧ Willow Chase ❧

#6 ❧ Ellen Elizabeth Hawkins ❧

#7 ❧ Alexia Ellery Finsdale ❧

#8 ❧ Evie Peach ❧

#9 ❧ Celou Sudden Shout ❧

#10 ❧ Summer MacCleary ❧

#11 ❧ Agnes May Gleason ❧

#12 ❧ Amelina Carrett ❧